I0656807

Herman L. Prior

Six Months Hence

being passages from the life of Maria Secretan - Vol. 3

Herman L. Prior

Six Months Hence
being passages from the life of Maria Secretan - Vol. 3

ISBN/EAN: 9783337332617

Printed in Europe, USA, Canada, Australia, Japan

Cover: Foto ©Andreas Hilbeck / pixelio.de

More available books at **www.hansebooks.com**

"SIX MONTHS HENCE."

BEING

SAGES FROM THE LIFE OF MARIA (née) SECRETAN.

> "Let them have scope ; though what they do impart
> Help nothing else, yet do they ease the heart."
> KING RICHARD III.

IN THREE VOLUMES.

VOL. III.

LONDON:

ITH, ELDER AND CO., 15, WATERLOO PLACE.

1870.

"SIX MONTHS HENCE."

CHAPTER I.

IT had come then at last, the terror of terrors! I was face to face with it; eye to eye: no disguise about it now. Hitherto I had cheated myself, hiding from my own view my own wretched weakness; just as a man might dissemble some malady at a banquet, until the fever-shudder has stricken the glass from his hand!

Even to the moment when I became aware of my husband's presence, my brain had busied itself with new combinations: how I should still go on with my task; how resolutely I would still guard the secret; how I would not be deterred from doing so by any puling anxiety for Helen's safety. But Mr. Fortescue's appearance on the scene scattered all this

to the winds. I cowered before him abjectly; without
purpose or helpfulness of any kind; neither praying,
nor deprecating, nor excusing: simply cowered.
Yes, indeed: the game was quite up now. Castle,
park, lands, coveted splendours of all kinds, they
signified no more to me than ingots would to a
drowning man. A century's lease of them would not
compensate the mortal fear of that one moment!

Happily, it was only a moment. My brain was
reeling under the shock: it must have succumbed;
but Mr. Fortescue spoke, and the relief was immediate.

His voice was intensely sad: touchingly so, as I
could not help observing even in my own agitated
state of feeling; but it was wholly free from anger or
menace of any kind: his ordinary voice and manner,
in fact, only with this added measure of mourn-
fulness.

"You have anticipated me," he said. "I came
here to fetch, and place in your hands, what you have
already taken possession of. How you discovered it I
know not; but it is of little importance now. I have
been here for some minutes," he added. "I left my
room when it had done striking twelve: when all
hope was quite over: quite over."

I ventured to look up at the speaker, and was further relieved by what I saw. The eye was wild and unsettled as it had latterly been, but there was no anger in it; on the contrary, its evident dejection told the same tale as the voice, appealing rather to pity and commiseration than any other feeling. He was completely dressed; as it seemed, in preparation for a journey of some kind. As I looked at him, I observed that he shivered.

"It is cold here," he said, "very cold; and I have much to tell you. We had better come up to my room : there is a fire there."

Although relieved from the extremity of my recent terror, I was wholly powerless to combat any proposition he might make. He led the way out of the "strong-room," and I went after him as a child or a dog might have done. The door of this room he closed behind us, apparently without paying any attention to its not being locked, and drew down the panel over it.

"That is right," he said, pointing to the steel cross, which I still held mechanically in my hands. "Keep that carefully; I will explain to you about it presently. It is hardly probable that it will be required;

but it may be. And now come upstairs. It is
singular how I feel the cold to-night."

On reaching the upstairs room, I saw that Mr.
Fortescue had not occupied the bed that night, notwithstanding his announced intention of retiring to
rest early. A tray with refreshments, of which he
had partaken slightly, stood on the table; beside it,
on the floor, was a small portmanteau, still open, but
with a few necessaries packed in it for travelling.

Courteously as ever, my husband placed a chair
for me, into which I sank with a feeling of intense
relief. There was a blazing fire on the hearth,
although the night was mild even for the time of
year. By this Mr. Fortescue seated himself, his right
side so close to the flame that I wondered it was not
scorched; but he did not seem to feel it.

Mr. Fortescue then commenced a narrative with
which I must deal as I best can.

I was instantly struck with his altered manner
in making it; something wholly different from the
wildness which had terrified me in his previous
disclosures. What he now said was minute, almost
wearisome, in its conscientiousness. It was the
penitent, labouring to disencumber his soul of the

guilt which oppresses it! Above all, even with an occasional tendency to wander, which increased as he proceeded, it was strangely *rational*, if I may use the term : startlingly so, after my experience of the last few weeks ;—after the death-agony of the last hour !

I hardly know how to present to the reader this detail, some portion of which is indispensable to the clearing of what has gone before. Much of what Mr. Fortescue said has been omitted; much of the rest condensed. If what remains is still given at too great length, I can only crave pardon for the over-fidelity of a memory which reproduces, in every word then spoken, the absorbing interest awakened by it at the time. Until their explanation came,—as it soon did come,—these utterances, over-exact as they may now appear, were among the most perplexing phenomena of the nature, so noble but so piteously overthrown, with which my life had linked itself.

My own mind, I should add, after the first shock was over, had become collected enough. I was determined to avail myself to the full of the revelations Mr. Fortescue was now disposed to make ; and which, as far as they lay within the region of fact, seemed to bear the stamp of truth. Even where

they were the evident creations of mania, they were
detailed (except for the tendency to ramble just noticed)
clearly and consecutively :—much as any ordinary
narrator would describe occurrences in which he had
himself borne part. When these wanderings occurred,
I found little difficulty in recalling the speaker to the
point from which he had diverged.

He began by a question ; pointing again to the
cross in my hand.

" You have seen that unhappy ornament before,"
he said. " You doubtless recollect who wore it ? "

I muttered some inarticulate assent, and he proceeded. " Oh ! Maria," he said, " it is terrible !
Maria, he . . . the boy to whom that cross belonged,
was our child! Let me try and nerve myself to
tell you.

" Even before I recognized,—although not before
I suspected,—what you had yourself been to me in
the past, I had made a still more agitating discovery.
You remember Fred's accident at the farm-house ;
when he broke his arm ? As you know, I carried him
home to the Villa, taking the shortest road, by the
cliff. In one place, the path skirted the brink for some
paces, descending into the sea sheer below us. As I

cautiously followed the track here, again there flashed
into my mind one of those marvellous intuitions of
identity. Not now for the first time had I borne on
a spot so perilous the helpless burden I was now
carrying! Once more, lying trustfully in my arms,
was the victim of my old remorseless act! Once
more I embraced my son!

"How I thenceforth watched over that young life,
you know; how unceasingly I tended him, day and
night, until the time of our engagement. But then I
became perplexed. His health promised to be
restored; but how was my right, my property in him,
to be secured? If I asserted the facts, who would
credit them; and what evidence could I produce?
Besides, I had a condition to perform. Of the
merciful purpose of this recognition I could not
doubt; it would end as happily as yours had done.
But before I could claim my reward, I must earn it:
I must save the life my rash act had once sacrificed!
Cold, cold, is it not, Maria?" he added suddenly,
laying his hand on the side which he still pressed
close to the blaze. "A curious kind of cold too; the
fire makes no difference to it: and it seems creeping
up me so. What can it be?"

A minute or two passed, during which Mr. Fortescue seemed only imperfectly conscious of what he
was doing. He then resumed his narrative—if the
wild combinations of his fancy in this portion of it
can be so called.

"Even in the deep happiness of our own union,"
he continued, "this anxiety pressed heavily upon me.
Before leaving Paris, I had matured an idea which
had several times previously crossed my mind. On
returning to England, I would again visit the spot
where I had received such revelations of the past.
There, as from an oracle, I would learn how this
matter was to end : would plead, if the performance
of this ultimate condition were not within my power,
that its necessity might be dispensed with !

"And this I did. You remember the journey
I took to Cumberland, the day . after we arrived
here ? "

How should I not remember it ?   I signified my
acquiescence, and he went on.

"I told you then," he said, " that my journey was
connected with my property in that county. But this
was not its real object. I went, not to adjust rent-rolls
and survey lands, but to explore once more, after the

lapse of so many years, the gloomy recesses of the
Scafell ravine! Oh! Maria, pity and pardon me! It
was the error of impatience! I should have waited for
Heaven's time :—I preferred my own. And now I
must pay the penalty!

"I slept at the house of the tenant I have before
mentioned, and reached Deep Ghyll by the same
route, and nearly at the same hour as when I last
entered it. A day, as intensely cold as that had been
sultry; the incessant drip of the rocks was arrested,
and the water stood on their swart sides in columns
and ribs of ice. The small strip of sky visible overhead there, at any time, was, on that day, of a
leaden hue, leaving the ravine nearly dark; while the
wind moaned in fitful gusts through its recesses.

"I bent my face on the stone pavement of the
chasm, bedewing it with salt, hot tears. Then I
pleaded aloud, with a passionate entreaty, 'May it
not be? I have not indeed saved that child-life; but
I have watched over it, shielded it from harm : so
wrought with it, that in its changed nature and dis-
position it is well-nigh a new existence. May I not
claim my reward ?'

"I was not left unanswered. The ravine in which

I knelt seemed to dilate. From its dark recesses issued a funeral procession, lit by torches, and bearing, side by side, two biers : one, thank Heaven, empty now; the other, still occupied by a childish form. I saw the memorial of my guilt, and again bowed my head in self-accusation. Slowly and interminably the procession wound upwards, while a bell tolled heavily overhead.

"Darkness again followed, and the bell ceased; but a reverberation from it still continued :—an independent sound, gradually articulating itself into speech. The words were low, but distinct beyond the suggestion of mistake.

"Their purport however was dark and mysterious.

"They spoke of a prayer granted, but granted only upon the strict terms of a condition; of a danger which now threatened that childish life; of the mode in which my agency might avert it; of the terms on which that agency would be employed.

"Lodged within the cavity of the heart; divided from its organic structure by only a thin membrane, was one of those entozoa frequently generated in the human frame, although rarely with such imminence of peril. Let the child-life proceed, and this life would grow with it; over-master it; extinguish it. Let the child-life be temporarily suspended, and this hostile agency would cease to exist.

" To one person only was it permitted to effect this :—to myself. Who had a more natural right ?

" The heart must be pierced: pierced to the core. Pierced ; but, as far as possible, without laceration : —some instrument must be procured, which would effect this. The blood flowing from the wound must be staunched, but no portion of it removed from the instrument used ; which must be taken away with me, as also the cross which the child wore round his neck: this cross.

" So far for the mere mechanical performance. But this was not all. Something more was required : —my faith. Absolute resignation of my own will. Absolute belief in the power which should restore the life apparently taken by my hand. Did I possess this ?

" Here was to be the criterion.

" My own agency in the matter was to be entirely secret :—the child's body, lifeless, as human science would have pronounced it, was also to be secreted in any way I might judge best. Immaterial this, after

all. However dealt with, nothing could retard its
restoration, if I had performed my part.

"The restoration. Yes. That was the all-
important matter :—and wholly my matter.

"At the end of forty-nine days from that on
which the wound was inflicted, I must begin to observe
the instrument used. Suddenly, between this and
the seventieth day, I should find it freed from the
rust of that blood ; clean ; bright. Easy enough the
rest then. Take the cross ; seek the child's body,
wherever deposited ; press firmly on the breast, on
the site of that cruel wound, the emblem of man's
life. Receive back its life. Possess.

"Ah ! Maria : but this was the programme for
success. This seventieth day was the extreme limit
possible. Should the instrument continue tarnished
at its close, the condition would not have been
fulfilled : — it would not be success, but failure.
Death to him :—anticipating, by a few weeks only,
the result which must in any case have ensued ; but
still, death by my hand.

"Death to him. To myself, ruin worse than all
death. Final, irretrievable. All that I had loved and
hoped for, in the past and in the future ;—all staked

upon one die; and lost. Do you follow me, Maria ? "

He saw by my face that I was listening intently, and resumed. " I must not lose time," he said. " There is still something to tell, and I feel a sort of confusion coming over me, which I never did before. Let me proceed while I can.

" I accepted the commission : I undertook that heavy charge; that ordeal of self-sacrifice. Had I not sinned, and must I not atone ?

" I again passed the night at the tenant's house, and early next day was on my way to Hastings. I had selected the necessary instrument meanwhile. Eastern touring had induced me to acquire some knowledge of surgery, which is in frequent requisition there ; and a small case of instruments has for many years been my habitual companion, even when not travelling. It contained what well suited the purpose ; a lancet, purchased in Aleppo, of unusual strength and keenness. Ah ! I cannot speak of that !

" Some disguise would also be wanted. I looked out an old fishing-dress which I had by me, not unlike those worn by the Hastings' boatmen ; I took this, and some few necessaries, with me. I did not put on the dress at once, but kept it to wear on arriving at Hastings.

"It was several days before I did so. The snow had not come on then; but my journey took a long time in-itself, as, to prevent being traced, I did not always follow the main roads. I had been required to be secret; and I determined to observe my directions to the letter.

"I was particularly careful about this after reaching London. Amongst other things, I took a seat, purposely booking myself in my own name, on the Hertford mail; on dismounting from which, I returned on foot during the night to the neighbour-hood of London : not entering the latter, but crossing the river into Surrey by Putney Bridge. I had also, in passing through town the day before, stopped at a small theatrical shop near Covent Garden, and bought some false whiskers. These I wore between London and Hastings, thinking it would be safer if I wore the two disguises separately. In this part of the journey too I also travelled entirely by unfre-quented roads; never stopping excepting at solitary houses or hamlets, and sometimes varying my

direction, so as to appear to be going towards
London. I don't know how I could have managed
all this so cunningly then, Maria. I couldn't now:
my head seems quite puzzled. Where did I tell you
I had got to?"

"You were making your way from London to
Hastings," I said.

"Yes," he said, "that was it. I got near Hastings
at last, to the north of the coach-road from there to
Battle. There was a thick copse by the side of the
lane in which I was, and which I knew joined the
turnpike road on top of the hill; here I put on my
fisherman's dress, and hid away the clothes I had
previously worn, in the hole of a tree. Having
secured them, I climbed the hill, and, crossing the
road, entered Hastings by the lanes on the Bexhill
side. The first flakes of snow fell as I did so. You
remember that great fall of snow then? It was still
lying, you know, when I got back here, only they
had cut through it. Do you remember how all the
mails were stopped?"

"Yes, yes," I answered. "But you were telling
me about Hastings. What did you do when you
reached it?"

" I forget," he said. " It is very strange. Oh:
yes; that was it: that little coffee-house behind
George Street. I got some refreshment there, and sat
till dusk reading the paper, without seeing any one
but the woman of the house. Then I again quitted
the town, and took the first field-path I came to; it
led me to that place in the stream:—Old Roar, you
recollect. It was frozen into icicles then. I needn't
have gone so far for concealment, as it soon came
on dark; but it answered the purpose. I waited
here some hours, at the foot of the waterfall, and
then walked back into the town again; which I had
some difficulty in doing: the snow however was
not in any deep drifts yet. The plan I had settled
was not to do anything until the following night.
That night, I had two or three things to ascertain:
—how I could best enter the villa; how the police
were stationed; where I could secrete the child, as
I had been directed to do. The latter occurred to
me as I now walked back to Hastings. 'Old Roar'
reminded me of our walk there with Mr. Latrobe,
and of what he told us of a disused communication
between his own room and the caverns on the West
Hill. I also recollected that, in some chance con-

versation at Paris, you had mentioned his going to
Ireland, and the insecure state in which his outer
door would be left : we laughed about it I recollect.
Well, on entering the town again, I crossed the
Castle Hill, and passed this door :—I found that it
opened, as you had said it would, with a very slight
pressure. The police arrangements too offered no
difficulty. You remember how Charles Armitage
used to take off the sergeant. Poor Charles ; poor
Charles! I wonder what he is doing now! Do you
know, Maria, I fancy——"

"You had better go on," I said. "Did you go
to the Villa that night ? "

"Yes. It was between three and four in the
morning, and I thought it would be better to take up
my position there at once. I walked round the
house several times, and then fixed on a place in the
shrubbery; near the side-door which you saw mentioned in the evidence :—the one by Mr. Armitage's
rooms. I knew that the key always hung up inside
there; Charles often went in and out that way,
leaving the door unlocked till his return. This
might give me the opportunity of entering the house
unobserved; and as the servants' offices, as well as

the hall-door, were on the other side, there was little
chance of my being discovered; especially with the
deep snow there was. I crept under a kind of bank
of snow, which I partially dug out for the purpose,
and waited for daybreak. Oh! but, Maria, it was
intensely cold. I knew it was at the time, although
I did not seem to feel it then; but I have felt
it at times ever since, creeping up me as I do now,
only it is so much worse to-night: it seems quite
to have numbed this side; and it is spreading up
the arm now, which I never felt before." As Mr.
Fortescue spoke, he drew himself still closer to the
fire, on which he piled fresh fuel. He then proceeded.

"Day broke at last: the struggling intermittent
light of a January morning. I partook of some
food which I had with me, and then set myself to
watch the house; making an aperture through which
I could at once see if the side-door opened: my own
hiding-place continuing wholly invisible, except upon
careful scrutiny. The snow still fell fast; thicker
and heavier than ever. I heard the gradual awakening of life indoors; movement and voices:— Fred's
voice, amongst others. He did not come out how-

ever; nor did any one approach the door I was watching. There seemed very little going on outside the house at all that morning. The snow was almost a *tourmente* in violence, and few cared to face it who were not compelled.

"At nine, the bell rang for the family breakfast, and at two for the servants' dinner. The interval had been wholly uneventful; and more than once I was on the point of abandoning my post, and entering by the hall-door. There would have been obvious risk in this however: besides, it would have interfered with the plan I had now formed, for concealing myself in Mr. Armitage's bed-room until night; when my object might probably be effected. So I remained where I was.

"It was weary waiting. At length, just as it fell dusk, the door was opened by the servant-girl whose evidence was taken at the inquest. All she said was correct. She and her lover stood talking at the side-door; an interminable time as it seemed to me. I became weary of this; and crept forward from my place of concealment to a new position, close to the door, so as to slip in unobserved if any chance offered. This I was able to do sooner than I expected. In moving, my foot caught in something which wrenched it, and drew from me an involuntary exclamation. As the girl said in her evidence, she thought this was some expression of impatience from her lover, from whom she had parted rather abruptly; and she walked a short way down the gravel-drive to him. Meanwhile, I entered the house unobserved.

"Here again, fortune favoured me. Mr. Armitage's room, I found, would not do;—the girl opened the door, apparently with the intention of going through it, although she changed her mind, and went back through the passage. This showed me that I was liable to interruption there : — perhaps even the room was occupied. I now thought of a bath-room on the other side of the passage, which I knew had been disused for a long time; the apparatus being out of order. I tried the door between this and the passage, but found it locked. The bath-room however seemed important to my purpose; and as there was another entrance to it,—just outside your old schoolroom, you recollect,—I resolved to try this. It was hazardous, as for this purpose I had to go into the hall and through the baize door

at the foot of the main stairs; but I thought it
worth the venture :—I knew, from the habits of the
family, that they would be dressing for dinner, and
no servants were likely to be about at that time.

"In a few seconds I had reached the hall, which,
as I expected, was empty; but just as I was crossing
over to the baize door, some one came out of your
school-room—Fred's nursery it was then, you know
—with a quick step, apparently intending to go
upstairs. I drew back immediately, and had not
time to see who it was, although the rustling of the
dress showed me it was a female. Whether I had
been seen myself, I could not be certain at the time :
I believed not; and this was confirmed by the
inquest, as, if I had been, it would of course have
been mentioned in the evidence.

"Meanwhile the person I had seen, instead of
proceeding upstairs, returned and went herself into
the bath-room passage : I heard the baize door swing
to behind her. This of course wholly prevented my
going there : in fact, my position was now one of
extreme difficulty, and required to be carefully
reviewed. I was hurrying back to the room I had
just quitted, when a new, and unexpected, actor

appeared on the scene. It was the little boy himself:
Frederick Poynder. He was quite alone; running
across the hall from the drawing-room door, which
had been left ajar.

" The whole thing had passed in a moment. Fred
had run out, almost stumbling against me, nearly at
the same instant that I had turned back after so
nearly being discovered. But there was my opportunity, and I at once used it.

" Catching up Fred in my arms, I pressed his
face firmly against my side, so as to prevent his
screaming, and at once carried him into Mr. Armitage's room. Here I adopted a more effectual mode
of preventing the child from calling for assistance,
as he would doubtless have done. The means were
for his own ultimate good, and I had no scruple in
using them. Foreseeing some necessity of the kind,
I had about me a bottle of strong extract, sufficiently
powerful, when dropped on a sponge and held firmly
to the mouth and nostrils, to suspend consciousness
for several hours. This I applied accordingly. In
doing so, the little fellow struggled, and some of the
fluid in the bottle was spilt on the bed by which I
stood; but, after this, he lay in my arms, wholly

passive and unresisting. I lost no further time, but
at once carried him out of the house, by the side-door,
to the shrubbery where I had lain so many hours in
concealment.

" Here a sudden thought struck me. It was
most desirable to avoid any discovery of the mode in
which Fred had been taken away. To insure this,
I left him, still wholly insensible, in the shrubbery,
and returned myself to the side-door, which I locked
on the inside, and hung up the key in the usual
place behind it. I then ran up to a sash window
which I saw above me on some back stairs leading
from the passage, and which I found unfastened;—
habitually so, as was clear from the state of the bolt.
To open this, and drop from it, shutting down the
sash after me, was the work of a moment; the
height was considerable, but the snow broke my fall,
and I sustained no injury. I then returned where I
had placed Fred.

" Having succeeded thus far, my next step was
to quit the grounds of the Villa with my burden.
The caverns could not of course be reached until the
night was far advanced; but meanwhile it was imperative to withdraw from the immediate neighbour-

hood of the house, as the child's absence must be
shortly discovered, and in all probability the police
would then be at once summoned. I therefore carefully effaced all traces of occupation from the shrubbery
where I had lain, and carried the boy, still wholly
unconscious, to a sheltered spot on the West Hill;
which, as you well know, rises immediately behind
the house. The latter I kept full in sight: in fact,
I was near enough to hear anything that might go
on there. Accordingly, carefully screening Fred from
the cold, I again sat and waited.

" The time seemed to me very long before anything unusual took place indoors; but it came at
last. All Saints' clock, close by me, struck seven,
followed by St. Clements, and the curfew. Then an
extraordinary commotion became at once visible.
Lights glanced from one window after another;
figures passed rapidly to and fro in front of them:
even through the closed sashes I could plainly hear
voices calling, and talking loud and eagerly. The
loss was evidently discovered! After apparently
exhausting every mode of search indoors, one or two
persons came to the front door, and peered out into
the darkness; but they did not go further, or send

for the police, as I had expected. On the contrary, they seemed satisfied that the child was in the house, and I could see that they were once more ransacking every corner of it. The lights then disappeared one by one, leaving only those which burnt in the rooms actually occupied. Evidently, the servants had now gone to supper:—I knew that would not be put off. I heard their voices in loud and excited discussion ; Burgess' shrill tones were distinctly audible.

" Once more, after supper, the search was renewed ; but, this time, with less spirit, and apparently by a fewer number of persons : renewed, of course, fruitlessly as ever. Once, the staircase window from which I had dropped was thrown open, and Fred's name was called by one of the women, in tones which made the hill ring again. He was lying hardly a hundred yards from the speaker, comfortably nestled in my arms !

" Lights now again appeared in some of the upper windows ; but stationary : the household was going to bed. By the time All Saints struck eleven, the whole of these were extinguished, with one exception ; Mrs. Armitage's, I concluded : she would still be brooding, in fruitless speculation, over the boy's disappearance.

"Again, a long, long watching. My companion still sleeping peacefully. Twelve o'clock sounded; one; two. It was time to act.—But you are weary of listening, Maria."

I begged him to proceed, which he did. "There is not much more now," he said, "and my head seems less confused; if only this numbing cold in the side would leave me. Let me see: it struck two, I told you."

"Yes."

"I rose from my hiding-place immediately afterwards," he continued, "effacing, as before, every trace of my having occupied it. Carrying the child, who was still insensible, I passed rapidly along the foot of the West Hill, skirted the church-yard, and looking anxiously up and down the London road, which was wholly deserted, crossed it to the broad footpath which you remember ran at the back of the High Street houses almost to the door of Mr. Latrobe's lodgings, so that I avoided the town altogether. When this footpath joined the one up the East Hill, I again looked anxiously up and down the latter; but

not a human being was in sight, or, judging by the
snow, had been near the place for hours. A few
moments carried me to Mr. Latrobe's door, which
opened as before. I ascended the stairs to his room;
and then the rest was easy work. I quickly removed
the skirting-board, and found the cellar underneath,
as he had described, with a door at the further end.
He told us the lock of the latter was rusted; and I had
provided myself beforehand with some oil to rub on the
key; as well as with a light and other necessaries. The
door, I found, did not open into the caverns at once, as
he thought it would; but this in the end answered my
purpose better. On traversing the passage, I found
that it terminated in an open archway; immediately
beyond which stretched some vaults, excavated in the
soil, and evidently connected with that portion of the
caverns shown to the public, although too mouldy and
insecure-looking to be actually part of the latter.

" It was the place and the hour for my appointed
work, and I hastened to it. Ah! but I cannot dwell
upon that, knowing what I now know. It was done,
Maria. Done, oh! how reverently; how submissively;
how tenderly to the childish frame I was thus
wounding for its own ultimate good! I put my

surgical knowledge to good use now. My instrument
pierced deftly and keenly : pierced to the heart. I
withdrew it, stained with a bright crimson. The blood
followed freely, and I staunched it ; propped the little
head on my knee ; received its last sigh as the lips
parted in death :—death, as it would have seemed.
I knew that the faculty of life remained suspended
only !

" My errand was despatched. I removed the cross
from the child's neck, and, kissing his forehead, carefully adjusted the body in the spot where I trusted it
would remain undisturbed, until I should come to
restore it to renovated being and health. On the
moulding of the archway above, I cut, in Malay—I
know not why, but the character, with which I was
familiar, casually occurred to me—the day of the
week and month ; so as to preserve them for reference,
in the unlikely event of my own memory failing me.
Then I retraced my steps along the passage ; replaced
the skirting-board as I had found it ; descended to
and closed after me the external door which had given
me such opportune admission ; crossed the hill to the
Ore lane ; joined the turnpike road. This I followed
to the lane by the side of which I had deposited my

ordinary clothes the day before. I found these as I had left them, and resuming them, made my way back to London; observing the same precautions as I had adopted in my journey to Hastings, and eventually entering town by a coach from a wholly different part of the country. This caused some further delay; and, as you know, it was some days before I rejoined you here.

"Yes: it was over. The task was achieved. Faultlessly, as regarded its appointed details: faultlessly, as regarded myself.

"Yes. I had triumphed. I had performed the condition; I had won the recompence. Terrible indeed, beyond human temptation, had been the ordeal! To bow my will to that stern decree; to lift my hand for *that* purpose; to deal a blow so cruel on the slumbering form beside me:—oh! Maria, I lived a life of agony in that one moment. But I bore it, humbly, meekly: it was my final retribution for the past; my complete restitution for the future. It was more; it was my child's life. I *trusted!*

"And yet; and yet—look here!"

As Mr. Fortescue spoke, he drew from his breast something carefully wrapped in a paper, which he removed. My eye followed him, shudderingly. It

was the fatal instrument he had described; the weapon
with which the maniac had equipped himself for the
death-stroke he was so unwittingly dealing!

" See here," he cried, pointing mournfully to the
steel, which was rusted and discoloured—" See here!
dull; dull; all dull: not one stain gone; not one
bloody witness wiped out. And yet this is the last
day: more than the last day. The seventieth day
really ended with the midnight preceding that which
struck just now: ended, as lawyers would compute
it. Ah! but was I to be cheated by their technicalities
and quibbles? I would have my full measure. It
was past midnight, long past, when I struck that
blow :—I was entitled to another twenty-four hours!
And now they are over too : and look—still dull,
still dull!

" Ay, Maria, and there is something duller still:
I know it now;—my wretched twice-duped self. I
would not admit the fact hitherto. Until the allotted
time was quite over, the mark quite overshot, there
was still hope.

" But for days past it has been the hope of desperation. I have clung to it like the drowning man's
plank, well knowing that it could not really bear me

over those tossing waves; that illimitable ocean! Yes, long since, even before the first period, the forty-ninth day, was over—even, I think, in the very moment of my fancied triumph—I heard a fatal whisper at my heart. Something even then told me that it was no victory I had achieved; but a cruel, cowardly act of bloodshed: that I was the victim of a cheat!—That the voice which spoke to me in that dismal chasm, was no messenger of good, but a false, lying spirit; one of those who in my long penance there, were ever seeking to trick, to cozen me: to make me the tool of their own accursed purposes. And now they have succeeded! Do you know, Maria," my husband continued after a moment's pause, and speaking in a hoarse whisper, "I sometimes of late think that I made too sure about that malady of my grandmother's. I am afraid sometimes now that I *am* mad: mad!"

The poor lunatic buried his face in his hands as he said this, and sobbed bitterly. After some minutes he looked up and spoke more calmly.

"Be all this as it may," he said, "I must bear the penalty of my own deed. And, first and foremost, I must see that others do not do so. I have carefully watched the newspaper accounts all this time, to see that there was no risk of this. Had there been, I know not how I could have observed the injunction not to disclose my share in this dark secret. Hitherto however no such contingency has occurred : —nothing beyond a temporary inconvenience, which would have been amply and easily atoned for had the event been what in my blind credulity I expected. But now, as you will see by the intelligence down-stairs, the matter is too pressing for a moment's delay. The cross now in your hand I wish you to retain as an additional security, in the event of any-thing happening to myself. Should this be the case, you must at once proceed to Hastings and detail the whole circumstances, so as to establish Helen's entire innocence. That unhappy trinket will be a sufficient voucher, should such be required, for the correctness of your statement. It is not probable however that you will have to do this. In half-an-hour hence the mail for London will pass the lodge gates ; I shall travel up by this, and then post to Hastings, where I shall at once deliver myself up to justice as the guilty party. I grieve for you, Maria," my husband con-tinued : "grieve deeply. I know the value you set upon our possessions here ; and now my life will be forfeited, and your tenure of them will be at an end. Gladly would I have spared you this, had it been possible. Very bitter as life would hereafter have been to me, darkened with the memories of the past, and still more with the hopeless and intolerable future, I would have borne it for your sake. But this cannot now be. The danger which menaces Helen Armitage must be averted immediately, and at all risks. Even the breath of suspicion should not rest upon her one moment longer. And now there is no time to spare for the mail. Farewell."

As Mr. Fortescue spoke, he closed the portmanteau, which stood on the floor, and was preparing to depart with it in his hand :—his left hand, I noticed.

Ah! but this should not be. During the latter portion of our interview, at any rate, mine had been the master-spirit of the two : the terror I felt at its commencement had been succeeded by a sense of power. I would stop this ruinous Quixotism : he should not leave the house as he proposed!—I sprung forward from my chair.

But his departure was arrested by a stronger arm than mine. As I moved, my husband turned from the door. Our eyes met, and in spite of my resolu-

tion, mine quailed before him. I was cowed once
more, and shrunk back into my chair, while he again
addressed me ; — gently enough. "Poor Maria,"
he said; "poor child ! Pardon me, if you can, this
heavy blow : pardon all the trouble and uneasiness
I have lately caused you. It was not. . . ."

The sentence remained unfinished. The strong
grip of paralysis was upon the speaker. The cold of
which he had been complaining told its own tale
now, and stretched him powerless and unresisting,
in front of the doorway where he had been standing !

CHAPTER II.

AFTER the first moment of surprise, I ran to Mr. Fortescue's assistance. The paralysis had affected the whole of the right side : leg, arm, and hand completely numbed, and the face drawn. I rang hurriedly for the servants, accounting for my presence in the room at this hour by some excuse connected with Mr. Fortescue's attack. Even in the confusion of the moment I did not omit to secrete the cross, which I had till now held in my hand, as well as the more fatal evidence of the crime which my husband had recently shown me.

Medical aid was not long in arriving. The surgeon who had been summoned was our own practitioner. He was a man of skill and intelligence, and I was well satisfied to leave the case in his hands; especially as he assured me, after a few hours, that it presented no unfavourable symptoms or complication of any kind.

"It was difficult to speak decidedly," he said, " so early in the attack ; but his own opinion was that the stroke, although severe in its immediate effects, was not one which threatened life. As far as he could judge at present, it was not constitutional, but something which had supervened :—an accident of the system, so to speak. Had Mr. Fortescue been subjected to any excitement, or undue mental strain, which could account for it ? "

I had considerable difficulty in replying to this. The case required wary walking. Powerless as I might have been to prevent my husband disclosing the secret, it should not be torn from *myself* by wild horses !

The invalid lay insensible on the bed before me. Not a soul in the house, in the whole world, knew, suspected, dreamt of, any portion of the facts. I answered, steadily and firmly, " No. None that I was aware of."

"I thought it possible," Mr Lankester continued. " However, there are other causes which will produce an attack of this kind, even when the system itself is not in fault. Mr. Fortescue has been an extensive traveller, I believe; and the drafts on the constitution made by exposure and fatigue often show themselves years after their actual occurrence."

I acceded to the surgeon's view gladly enough. After some hours' attendance he left the Castle, promising to return in the forenoon. It was daybreak by this time.

Mr. Lankester paid his promised visit, and another in the evening of the same day. My husband continued insensible : apparently, he was in the same state as he had been ever since the seizure. But I fancied that in Mr. Lankester's face I now detected an expression of uneasiness ; something of a puzzled look. I was unable to refrain from questioning him as to this.

" You are a quick observer," he answered. " I am free to confess that since I was here last night some indications have shown themselves in the case which I cannot quite account for. They are hardly capable of being stated with any definiteness, and I do not know that of necessity they are unsatisfactory ; but they perplex me. There is some great change going on in your husband's system. Quietly and tranquilly as he lies to all outward appearance, there is in reality something at work which, should he recover,—as I make no doubt he will—will in some form or another produce a marked alteration in him. Not of necessity a serious alteration. The action itself is violent; abnormal; but its results may not be proportionably so. It may affect temperament, bodily habits; operate in twenty different ways, all wholly unimportant. But there the fact is. And now I must wish you good evening. I will be here the first thing to-morrow. Should consciousness return, you will of course send for me at once."

Another day's watching. No return of consciousness. The sufferer still lying numbed and insensible; breathing, but, to my unpractised eye, showing no other indication of life. The medical attendant still watching him with that curious puzzled look: still, when questioned, speaking of this internal struggle; this singular change, as he still called it, at work; something wholly imperceptible to myself, but patent to the quick glance of science.

Again Mr. Lankester quitted me, with the promise to be back at the Castle early on the day following;

directing me, as before, to send for him should
anything of importance occur during the interval.

I had procured some necessary sleep during the
day, and now again lay down for an hour or two. I
then returned to the sick room, where I dismissed
my maid Forbes, and took my post by the bedside.
The other servants had all been sent to rest. Forbes
slept near at hand, ready to be summoned if
required.

Ten o'clock, eleven, struck successively ; then
twelve. Just forty-eight hours from the time at
which I had discovered the concealed drawer in
Mr. Fortescue's strong-room, and drawn from its
hiding-place the witness of his fatal act. How much
had happened since then ? And what was to be the
sequel now ?

Not death : that the surgeon had assured me.
And in that fact there was unspeakable relief. The
more violently my hold upon the coveted prize of my
life was shaken, the more tightly I clenched hand
and grip upon it. I could not have borne that it
should be wrested from me.

To this extent however, it seemed I was at least
safe. But what safety ? What was this prolonged

life to be? The endurance of the last few weeks;
the concentrated agony of that, their closing day?
Could I live this life out?

As I thus pondered, I was startled by a sound
from the bed. Mr. Fortescue moved. I rose and
stood facing him. He had begun to speak;—articulate
words, although in the surprise of the moment I
failed to gather what they were. A request for water,
I fancied; but I was not sure : whatever it was, the
sentence was left incomplete. The speaker sat up in
bed, and looked at me with an expression of utter
bewilderment.

" Miss Secretan ! " he exclaimed.   " Good
Heavens ! What . . I mean, what has happened?
I hope this is not my fault, in any way. Where
am I ? "

Something in Mr. Fortescue's voice had arrested
me in the first words he uttered. Something in his
eye, as he now sat fronting me, did so still more
powerfully.

Again, " was this possible ? "

Had I lost my senses ? Or, had he recovered
his ?

Possible.   Quite possible.   Quite true.   One

moment's glance, and I had no more doubt of the
fact than I had of my own identity. The eye which
had met mine forty-eight hours since; the eye before
which mine had quailed, in spite of itself, at the
moment of his seizure, longing passionately to find
some mode of retarding his purpose and yet not
daring to do so, had been that of a madman. The
eye on which I now looked, although it wore a
confused and troubled expression, was that of absolute sanity: something which I had never seen in
my husband before. Something which told me, by
the instinct of a reciprocated intelligence, that the
mind which now spoke through it, however enfeebled
by recent occurrences, was essentially one of the same
order as my own; intelligent, apprehensive; the seat
of reason, reflection, order!

Ah! when Mr. Lankester spoke of the "constitutional change" which he believed to be going on
in his patient, how little had he thought of what his
words really imported! How hard to realize it, even
now!

And yet, so the fact was. The hereditary taint
transmitted from that foreign ancestress, had done
its work. But it had done it only partially. Im-

pinging on the brain at some past period,—when, I
had never exactly gathered,—it had distorted and
marred it; filled it with the delusions of unreality,
haunted it with spectres; driven it on its erratic
course into violence and involuntary bloodshed. But
here the malady had worn itself out. Such agency
as the mind could still exert, such impressions as
it was still capable of receiving, would be freed from
this disturbing influence. They would be the acts
and thoughts of a sane man!

Thus far I had considered the matter as it affected
Mr. Fortescue: at least, if that can be called consideration which shot through my mind, almost
while he yet spoke, with the flash of intuition.
But equally rapid and instantaneous was another
speculation: how did the change affect myself?

How should it, except in a way to cause me
boundless satisfaction? Mr. Fortescue's life, and
Mr. Fortescue's reason were the two sheet-anchors
by which I held on to all I prized and coveted, in the
past, present, and future. Now, here was life safe,
as the doctor assured me. And here, as I assured
myself, was reason restored also. That second
anchor, after dragging helplessly all these weary

weeks, had found something to hold it at last. The
fatal clause in the settlement was cancelled : it was
as though it had never existed !

My heart throbbed wildly with these new emotions.
But meanwhile it was necessary to reply to my
husband's wondering inquiries, as well as to summon
Mr. Lankester. The latter I attended to first, directing Forbes, who awoke at my first call, to dispatch
one of the grooms to the post-town, and await his
return herself downstairs. This done I moved gently
to the bed, and took my husband's hand. The whole
had passed in infinitely less time than it has taken
in relating.

"You do not know me," I said ; "and it is
hardly wonderful, after the severe illness you have
had. But Miss Secretan is not my name now. See
if you cannot recall something else about me : something which gives me a right to be here ? "

It was an anxious moment. I did not know how
far this confusion of the now sane faculty might
extend, or what future entanglements might result
from it. But I was quickly re-assured. Some
recollection of the past struck the required chord,
and I saw the face at once brighten into intelligence.

"Maria!" Mr. Fortescue exclaimed. "Good Heaven, what was I thinking of? I have been ill: light-headed or drowsy or something; and when I woke just now my mind went back to Hastings. Has anything happened?" Mr. Fortescue added, after a pause, during which he threw a startled look round the room.

"Nothing," I said, "excepting that you have had a serious attack, and Mr. Lankester has been attending you. He will be here again soon. And now you must not talk, or exert yourself in any way."

"Nothing has happened then?" Mr. Fortescue repeated, disregarding my injunction. "I am glad of that. When I woke up, I had the feeling upon me that there had been something very dreadful: I have no idea what; but some great disaster, for which I was responsible. I am glad that it is not so. Do you know, Maria," he continued, after again pausing, and looking round the room, as if to fix some definite object, "I feel as if I had been living in a dream. I know that we are married, of course; but I cannot at all recall when or where. And that time at Hastings, all that seems a dream too. I remember some things in it, but forget others ; and I seem to forget everything since it, altogether. My head feels so weak, so confused."

" You had not better try it further now," I said. " Lie down, and I will sit by you without talking until your doctor comes : it will be best thus."

Mr. Fortescue complied with little resistance. The effects of the seizure were evidently passing off ; —movement restored, or nearly so, as well as speech. But the state was still that of prostration, both in mind and body.

Would this last ? I sat pondering. Especially, would it last as regarded the mind ?

This latter was all-important. Already my intense delight in the restored prospects opened out by my husband's recovery of reason was dashed with apprehension. True, this would prevent the fatal clause of forfeiture from operating in the future ; but could it undo the past ? The conditions of forfeiture had already arisen : fatally and irrevocably. True again, at present I was the sole depository of the secret. But how long should I remain so ?

Poisoning all my joy, quenching every spark of

renewed hope, came that intolerable thought,—
Helen ! If memory returned ; if the dark tragedy
of the Hastings caverns came back to Mr. Fortescue's
mind, vivid in detail as it had been immediately
before his seizure, or even in some form only of
confused recollection, was it not certain how he
would act ? If the lunatic was so studious for
that girl's safety, would not the sane man endorse
the solicitude twenty times over ? Would not his
very first act be to secure her liberation ;—and
his own incarceration as a criminal lunatic ? A
pleasant prospect, truly ! Dalemain might as well
be entombed by an earthquake, as far as I was
concerned !·

But then, my husband might not recover his
memory ; at any rate of these recent occurrences.
That was my one hope, and I clung to it with the
energy of despair. What my own course was to
be if this did prove to be the case—if the sick
man's memory did serve me this good turn — I
did not analyze very carefully ; but I thought
I knew.

" My reveries were disturbed by Mr. Fortescue
again speaking. " Maria," he said, gently. I rose

and stood by his side. "Maria," he repeated, "did you do right in marrying me? Why did you? I ought to have married Helen; Miss Armitage: I must have wronged her shamefully. And what did I do it for? Maria, have I been mad?"

The crisis was appalling. In any moment the brain might recover its lost clue, and then, fire and water would not restrain him from making the disclosure. I summoned all the nonchalance I could to my assistance.

"Mad!" I echoed. "No, certainly not. But you will make yourself really and seriously ill, in some form or another, if you persist in exerting yourself. You should not speak; not think, if possible."

"It is not much use my trying to do so, certainly," he said. "I feel as if I was on some height, trying to discover the objects round me, but interrupted by a driving mass of cloud and mist: and the cloud seems growing blacker and deeper every moment. Ill, ill; very ill. Ill here," he murmured, passing his hand over his forehead: "something wrong here." He then sank off into a heavy sleep.

Mr. Lankester arrived soon afterwards, but would not disturb his patient. I told him shortly what had occurred; of course with the necessary reservations. He then sate and watched with me by the bedside.

It was long after daybreak, the March sun darting a pencil of light through an opening in the drawn curtains, before Mr. Fortescue woke. The doctor had requested me, when this should occur, to leave him alone with my husband, and I did so. He could judge better of him, he said, by quietly observing his patient for a few minutes without the foreign excitement which my presence would naturally cause : he would at once communicate to me the result.

How feverishly I waited for that result to be announced! My fate trembled in the balance. My husband might have awoke with perfectly restored faculties : might, at that moment, be telling the doctor the whole story ! Oh ! Heaven !

I quivered in every nerve with impatience. I would have played the eaves-dropper at the bedroom door ; but the servants were often by there, and I did not dare. There was no help for it, but to sit in my turret boudoir, waiting, waiting ; looking out on the glorious expanse of dale and woodland and bright water as if it were the green curtain of a theatre !

At length the expected sound came : Mr. Lankester knocked lightly at the door, and entered. He was very grave.

. " I have detained you a long time," he said; " but it was of the utmost consequence, with a view to your husband's future treatment, that I should at once ascertain the state in which his attack has left him. Mrs. Fortescue, I must prepare you for a very great shock. I fear the mind is permanently enfeebled. I told you of an internal struggle, a constitutional change of a very marked kind, which I observed going on in him during the last two days. I was not without my own apprehensions as to the issue of this; although it would have been cruel to have distressed you by an earlier statement of them : I grieve to say that they have now been fully verified. The brain, whether originating the attack or not, has sympathised with it to an extraordinary degree :—the struggle, so to speak, has culminated there. And the result is that while the physical power of the system remains, as far as I can judge,

unimpaired, the mental condition is greatly altered.
Your husband may live for years, and be as strong
and active as ever ; but the mind can never, I fear,
be what it has been.   It seems perfectly sound and
free from delusion of any kind ; but it is feeble :
the apprehension dull, the memory confused and
defective ; especially, I find, as to recent occurrences.
Pray believe, Mrs. Fortescue," the doctor added
kindly, " that I have extreme pain in saying this.   I
could not have borne to do so excepting in the
discharge of a duty, which I observe in all cases of
illness ; that of telling the sufferer's friends, at any
rate, the entire truth."

" Extreme pain ! "   " Could not have borne to
tell me ! "   The speaker little suspected the tempest
of joy which each successive word of his roused
within me !

Better and better every moment ! Ah ! truly,
had the veil of my thoughts been lifted but for
one moment, the surgeon would have spared his
sympathy ! He would have fled aghast and dis-
mayed from the leprosy of further contact with the
wife he was compassionating !

Little indeed did he guess that what he described

as Mr. Fortescue's enfeebled state of mind was in fact an improvement, huge as the difference between life and death, on the conditions of its former mania. But, still less could he guess the deep reason I had for rejoicing that the improvement had exhibited itself in this qualified form only! In a form which would place my husband henceforth wholly in my power, instead of placing myself and my fortunes in his!

Some answer was necessary however, and by a strong effort I succeeded in masking my feelings sufficiently to make it. Not only masked my feelings, but already, in the minute or two's silence which ensued, shaped out the rudiments of a plan for utilizing this new state of facts. The doctor, good man, set down the delay to wife-like emotion, and sat pitying me accordingly!

"You have done right, Mr. Lankester," I said at last, in a low tone. I dared not trust my voice higher, lest its exhilaration should break out in spite of myself and give the lie to my own words!

"You have done quite right," I said. "I am obliged to you for having thus told me the truth, as well as for the sympathizing and friendly manner in which you have done so. I almost feared this result from what I had observed myself. But it is the ruling of a higher power, and I must bear it as I best may."

"I trust you may be strengthened to do so," the doctor replied.

"I will endeavour," I said. "And now it is to the sufferer himself that our whole attention must be directed. Mr. Lankester, you will think the suggestion I am about to make rather a wild one : and, of course, I speak wholly without medical knowledge ; but it did occur to me, while waiting for you, that some change might be desirable for him ;—of course, as soon as it could be safely effected. Even the memory, on which, as you say, the brunt of the attack has fallen, would be more likely to recover its tone in new scenes, than here at home. What do you think ? "

"I agree with you entirely," Mr. Lankester answered. "I should have made the same proposition myself in a few days, and am glad you have anticipated me, as it will allow of your plans being formed earlier. Immediate change of scene is the *very* best thing for Mr. Fortescue : the best, I fear

almost the only chance of his mind regaining its
tone. And the general health is already so greatly
restored that there will be no difficulty about this.
With the exception of a stiffness in the right arm,
which I apprehend will not be of long continuance,
he has entirely shaken off the attack. He must have
an excellent constitution. Yes," continued the
doctor, after a moment's reflection, " if you are really
disposed to undertake the journey, and can arrange
for it so soon, I think that you might leave, say, on
the third day from this, very well."

" I can so arrange it," I said. " Where do you
think we should travel ? "

" It is hardly material," answered Mr. Lankester.
" The change itself is the great thing."

" The continent," I suggested.

" Yes, better than anything. You will of course
travel by easy stages ; fatigue of any kind should be
avoided. In his present condition, I imagine,
Mrs. Fortescue, you will find your patient entirely
submissive : your will will be a law to him.
Sad as his present state of mind is, it has this
advantage."

" It has," I thought to myself.

I thanked the doctor warmly for his sympathy and counsel, and our interview terminated. Leaving me at liberty to shape out my plans for the further tragedy I now avowedly to myself contemplated.

CHAPTER III.

"The further tragedy I now avowedly contemplated!"

Yes. It had come to this.

Why had I suggested this foreign tour? Why had I caught so eagerly at Mr. Lankester's acquiescence? Why, but because I dared not remain in England, resolving as I had resolved.

I had to look matters in the face now. The dilemma required no logical statement, no balancing of reasons; it was simple and straightforward enough. Here was a crime committed; inquiry set on foot; the actual perpetrator unknown and unsuspected; the innocent charged; the charge, thus far, established. How indeed this result had been brought about I had no knowledge. On my memorable visit to Mr. Fortescue's room, two days before,

my eye had been caught by the large type in which
the newspaper stated Helen's committal for trial;
but I had no time to read the details. Now, I preferred not doing so : there was the fact, and that
was all I had to deal with. The more algebraically I
could do so, divesting it of all personal elements,
the better.

Just on this wise. Let the party thus charged,
and standing for trial at the assizes,—as I knew, a
week or two hence,—be A. B. That would answer
all purposes. That was A. B.'s position : what was
mine ? In my breast,—and, in Mr. Fortescue's
present state, in mine only,—rested the knowledge of
the facts which demonstrated A. B.'s entire innocence. With me, and with me only, was lodged the
power of at once establishing it. Did I intend to
do so ?

No. No. A hundred times no. What ! after all
I had endured—had been preparing myself further to
endure, to give up the game just when endurance
ceased to be necessary ?—When the path lay smooth
and clear before me; no disguises required, no
detection always imminent; no maniac's society to
be undergone; no charge or anxiety but that of

watching over an enfeebled brain, wholly subservient
to my wishes :—not even enfeebled beyond the point
which was necessary for preventing its recollection of
certain unpleasant facts ? Was it tolerable that I
should do this ? Why, if I had planned for the purpose, plotted against my husband's health, drugged
him, steeped the poor crazed brain in deadening
essence or paralyzing odours, I could not have arrived
at a more satisfactory result than what had now
happened. And now, when the result had come to
me, free and unsolicited, was I a baby to throw it
away from me ?

At the same time, this alternative was not a pecu-
liarly comfortable one. So far from comfortable, that
once or twice, when it presented itself in its naked
simplicity—even as a matter between myself and
A. B. merely—the beads of perspiration stood on my
forehead with merely thinking of it. I devoutly
wished the assizes had not been so close. Two weeks
only ! It had such a practical look. Supposing that
. . . well, that life were forfeited, who would have
taken that life ? What, in plain language, would
society call the person who had done so ? And,—
would the law do the same ? A murderess ? No.

Ridiculous! What penalty did I incur by simply keeping to myself certain facts which I knew, and no one else did? Where was the obligation to proclaim my husband's history in the market-place? Was I town-crier?

Still the thought haunted, hunted me: it came baying upon me, open-mouthed. When I talked of law, it spoke of the inner tribunal of conscience: the lash and thong ever sounding in that gloomy chamber; the foreshadowed doom beyond it!

Ah! I might, after all, have yielded: might have escaped the terrible end! But it was not to be.

When some joint or nerve is rudely impinged upon, nature throws out a protecting medium. When unpleasant truths come home to one, as they do now and then come home in spite of all effort and precaution, the mind does the same. Give but time: let the conviction fail, but for five minutes, in producing the action which is its final cause, and we begin to fortify ourselves against the next attack. Fool that I was to torment myself thus! What chance was there of Helen being convicted? True, innocent persons had been convicted before now, often enough. True, I had not read the depositions;

had no intention of doing so; did not know, and should
not, what apparent proofs had come to light; what facts
might be welded together into that chain of circumstantial evidence which has so often, and so mysteriously
proved a lying prophet—brought home guilt to the
door, tracked it into the bed-chamber, fastened it on
the palm of those who in reality have all the time been
innocent even of its suggestion! True, this might be
so now. But I did not know it: did not intend to
know anything about it. Wait and see, at any rate.
At the worst, there would be ample time afterwards;
long before anything serious could happen.

I recollected another matter too :—the allusions
which, when suspicion first became excited against
Helen, had been made to her subsequent delirium.
I had read these in the Hastings' papers at the time,
and now found my advantage in having done so. Of
course! Why, let the charge, by some chapter of
accidents, be proved even against Helen, and here
was safety! No one would dream of holding her
responsible, under the circumstances. Some temporary inconvenience, some trouble and perplexity ;
that was about the outside of the mischief. Not
more, after all, than Mr. Fortescue himself would be

subjected to, were I to disclose the real actor in the
tragedy.   He too would have to be defended on the
same ground of 'unsound intellect.' Quite as long
as it was broad. Ah! I would have nothing to do
with it.   Things must take their course.

So I juggled myself to my own destruction. So I
stopped my ears, and buried my head under the
clothes, while the booming water leapt on, and the
walls already shook with its approach!

One thing only I could not do : I could not stop
at home and see the result. Not stop in England
even, if I could help it. Something at my heart all
the time told me that I was best out of the way when
the trick—for I knew it was juggling—was played out.

Perhaps there was a deeper motive still :—the
fixed, although unavowed purpose of putting any
change, in any event, *out of my power?*

CHAPTER IV.

THE Continent?

Yes. And the remotest corner of it to which I could penetrate.

We had not been able to travel fast, however. Mr. Fortescue's bodily health was much restored, but it would have been imprudent to incur any excessive fatigue, and our journey was made in moderate stages accordingly. We had quitted Dalemain on the day named by Mr. Lankester, travelling *en route* for Switzerland; but at the end of a week we had only reached Basle.

Its bustle accorded ill with my companion's state, and suited mine still less. Quitting the hotel on the Rhine-swept quay after a hasty refreshment, we again pushed forwards.

The peaks of the Oberland and Chamounix throw

forward an advanced guard in the Jura ; a range much humbler in elevation, and gloomy rather than imposing. Here and there however the monotony of this hill barrier is broken by scenes of beauty and interest. The Munster Thal, lying between Basle and Bienne, is one of these. The limestone rocks are cleft by a stream of bright water, from the bed of which they rise fantastically grouped, and clothed with picturesque creepers. It is a spot which, although it cannot compete with the Alpine valleys, is often recalled with pleasure even after the traveller has become familiarised with the latter. On my jaded heart and eye it acted with a powerful charm.

Urged forward incessantly as I was, panting in the hopeless flight from that worst pursuer, self, I still had need of rest; and the peaceful glen, with its meadows and sparkling river, secluded by the rock-parapet which bounded it from all communication with the outer world, arrested my steps in spite of myself. I decided on remaining there some days, and engaged rooms accordingly at an hotel situated in a picturesque part of the valley, which here formed nearly a right angle. My husband seemed pleased with any arrangement I chose to make.

Mr. Fortescue had gained strength daily; but I could detect no alteration in his mental state. The mind continued wholly free,—permanently free, as I was quite satisfied,—from the disease which had so long preyed upon it: as far as its power went, it was now an entirely sound mind; but the power was greatly limited. He conversed, often with interest; read books and papers; enjoyed the scenery, of which he was always a passionate admirer. But he seemed strangely absorbed in the present: no question was ever asked about our journey, our intended movements: no reference made to any subject of a personal nature: no inquisitiveness as to his illness, as to why we had left Dalemain; why we were here. He accepted everything as it came, just as a child might. It was not at all times too that he was capable even of the mental effort thus required. He often dozed through a good part of the day: dozed; or sat, or lay on the couch, apparently dozing.

All this was well: especially well that there should be this broken link between our present and former life. The memory seemed gone; or, if it still existed, it was so dim and confused, as to be practically in abeyance. Whether the dark shadow of something in the past still hung over it, I could not tell. Perhaps it did, forming an additional reason why he thus abstained from all personal reference.

But, let this be as it might, it was evident that the faculty itself was greatly impaired. The paralysis, as Mr. Lankester had said, had culminated in this quarter.

The state of things, therefore, as regarded my husband, was now all I could wish : suitable to my present plans and intentions ; full of good augury for the future. It had only to continue ; and it gave every promise of doing so. Should the promise be fulfilled, we might then, after some pleasant months abroad, return to Dalemain, and resume life under altogether improved conditions. The past would be a hideous dream, which the palsy had already swept out of the recollection of the main actor in it ; and which, if I knew myself, I should have no difficulty in keeping at a safe distance from mine.

So I argued, whenever I reflected upon the matter calmly and reasonably. I had a right to be happy now: why should I not ? Let me be so then : —enjoy this tranquillity, these fair scenes !

All very delightful in theory. But in execution

there was one untoward element which spoiled all. That girl : Helen. She haunted me : positively haunted. It was unbearable.

Mr. Fortescue is dozing now; let me go out; take my book; my sketching materials. What can be lovelier than this day? What more picturesque than this miniature gorge; more musical than its waters; more peaceful than its one road, traversed two or three times in the twenty-four hours by the diligence or the carriage of some occasional visitor, but ordinarily left to its own traffic : the waggons of the peasantry, and the sledges in which the ore dug in the valley is conveyed to the forges in which its artisans carry on their humble manufacture? What had Helen to do there?

But eternally she was there. Occupying a seat in those chance carriages; riding among the country people in the waggons. Starting from the broken rocks in the stream; from the way-side chapels; from every bend and corner of the road. Climbing with a slow step some green slope on the further side of the valley. Glancing between the stems of the hanging pine-woods. Frowning down upon me from the quaint pinnacles of the limestone cliff. Shutting out all light, all joy, all rest!

Oh ! it would pass : it would pass ! Why should
this trick of the brain thus scare and terrify me ?
Why should it grudge me this short happiness ?
What did it mean too by passing that further cheat
upon me; changing and shifting as it did—sometimes
being Helen, and sometimes not Helen, but some
one else : a face and form, recollected, alas ! but too
well ? What made it, at last, altogether cease to
represent Helen, and wear that other semblance—
uniformly and exclusively ? What had *he* to do
with it ?

I bore this : bore it for two whole days. It
required nerves of iron ; but I *would* do it.

The third day rose, like its predecessors, bright
with sunshine, soft with tender shadows ; scented
with the breath of the spring flowers. To me alone,
how intolerably dark and gloomy !

But the day did not terminate as its predecessors
had done.

Throughout the entire forenoon the presentiment
of some great evil hung over me. I tended Mr.
Fortescue as far as his convalescent state now needed
it ; read and talked to him ; accompanied him for
a short walk in the woods behind the hotel, to which

his strength was now adequate. How I envied his happy light-heartedness. He was full of conversation and interest on every object, feeling the beauty which surrounded us with the intensity of a man just recovered from a long sickness : and apparently without the least vestige on his mind of the shadows which had so long haunted it; still less of the terrible secret of which we two were the sole possessors. Much as if he were a child, placed in some elysium of being, with faculties for enjoying it to the highest degree, but without antecedents or future of any kind. The terrible gulf had been bridged over; the boy's heart was now come back again, with its frank gaiety, its heedlessness of all but the interest of the passing moment !

Then Mr. Fortescue returned to the hotel to doze; which he still did a good deal. And then the overpowering apprehension which my attention to him had served to dissipate, settled down upon me in a darker and heavier cloud than ever.

It wanted at least two hours to the table d'hôte. It seemed as if this interval would be an age. It was not *ennui* I felt; the weariness of a self without resources; the imperative need of something to kill some inevitable interval. This was a need I had never experienced, and I did not now. Plenty of avocation round me ; plenty of sights and sounds to interest, employments to settle to with zest, if this foreboding which beset me had only permitted it !

But it would not. I could no more have turned to any ordinary occupation than a man could hum tunes on his way to execution : I *dared* not. Something warned me that a crisis in my being, great and terrible as that of dissolution itself, was about to take place. I must not fail to meet it : not be out of the way, be frivolously or lightly occupied, when it did come. What was to come, and whence, and how, I had no knowledge : no introvision. But I sat waiting : every faculty strained for the arrival of the actual presence which threw before it this dark shadow.

I sat at first in my own room ; quite motionless : occupying the couch on which I had placed myself after leaving Mr. Fortescue.

Then, I wandered out into the hotel garden for air, and sat down on one of the benches there ; motionless as before : seeing nothing, thinking of nothing ; simply waiting.

Then the bench nearest me was occupied by other visitors; a good-natured and loquacious German party. I rose, and slowly ascended the hill of the village above the hotel. Accident rather than purpose led me to the churchyard; a terraced ground with a low parapet wall and seats, commanding exquisite views up and down the valley. I again seated myself; looking at the views; seeing nothing.

And then, in that peaceful enclosure, in the face of those bright meadows, that gleaming water, that blue sky, my doom was spoken. The watched-for and the watcher stood face to face !

The sound of voices entering the churchyard; of steps on the path behind me. I turned, and saw no one that I knew. Two young Englishmen; one rather the elder of the two, but probably neither yet more than twenty : gentlemen as I saw at a glance. They moved to the parapet wall at some little distance from me, and leant over it admiring the prospect.

"Worth the climb, was it not?" said the younger of the two. "There is some air too up here. Isn't it like the old place?"

"The old place?"

"Yes, Harrow churchyard, you know: the view from Byron's tomb, as we used to call it."

"Well, Harrow is on a hill, and this place is in the middle of a valley; perhaps however, with some stretch of imagination one may see a resemblance : this wall ought to be railings though."

"Do you often go down there?" asked the first speaker.

"Never, hardly. The office work is extremely heavy now that my father's partner has retired, and it is almost impossible to get away. I should not have been here now but for some foreign evidence they want in a Chancery suit, which the manager thought I could get better than any one else. You're the lucky fellow, Powell; lots of money, and nothing to do but to go about and amuse yourself. Singular, was it not, our meeting in this out-of-the-way place? I suppose you have been up all the mountains here?"

"That's a large order," answered the younger speaker. "I tried a few of them last summer, but it's too early yet for mountain work. I am going into Italy. By the way, talking of Harrow, have you seen this about Armitage?"

"Armitage?"

"Yes, don't you remember? He was in the shell when we were there : he was captain of the eleven afterwards."

"Oh! of course. Nice young fellow he was, too. But what has happened?"

"Why you remember that murder at Hastings in the winter :—a boy that was stolen out of some house there, and the body found afterwards concealed in an underground cavern there?"

"Yes, no doubt. But what had Armitage to do with it?"

"Oh! don't you know? The child was his step-brother; at least not that either : the child's mother married his father."

"Really! Was that his sister then who was committed for trial on the charge the other day? I saw it before I left England, but the name did not strike me."

"Yes, that was Armitage's sister. An uncommonly pretty girl too : met her at Hastings once. I never believed for a moment she was guilty : a girl couldn't have done such a thing as that."

"I should think not. But what about Armitage himself?"

"Why it seems some evidence has just turned up, which brings the murder home to him beyond dispute. I don't know what it is, for there is only a short notice in *Galignani;* but I am afraid it must be true. They say he was committed at once, and will be tried at the assizes next week."

"Ah! yes; at Lewes that will be. The assizes there are unusually late this spring; there has been so much business on the rest of the circuit. But what a shocking thing! What can have been the motive?"

"I am afraid there was only too much. I remember the newspapers at the time spoke of Armitage's father having made a will cutting him out of everything if the child attained twenty-one. But he seems not to have been suspected until now. *Galignani* says the people thereabouts are furious with him for allowing his sister to be charged without coming forward himself."

The conversation continued; but I heard no more: I fled from the churchyard. I felt as I did so, that both speakers were directing upon me a gaze of wondering speculation. What mattered it?

I had never dreamt of this: never dreamt of it!

I must be up and stirring instantly, at any price.
Let them look; if only I could get forward. But
oh! how hard that was! How my limbs shook
under me: how palsy-stricken knee and foot
seemed, as I forced them to do my bidding!

Quickening my walk, step by step: quickening it
to a run as I reached the further end of the enclosure.
Down the hill: into the hotel: to my own room
upstairs. To the discovery of my own new self!

Ah! I had no heart, had I? So I had always
thought: taken it for granted. But I had one,—I
had found it out now:—a passionate woman's heart;
throbbing to its core with the love which I had so
forcefully thrust back, and which now turned upon
me like a beast of prey, hungry and open-mouthed!
Should I be in time to save him? Might it yet be—
oh! might it? I had no thought, no consciousness
but this. Mind and soul were swallowed up in it!

Yes. In one instant I had torn from my eyes
the veil of self-deception. Torn from my breast the
demon-forms which haunted it: the covetousness, the
greed of wealth and self-indulgence! I could have
lavished all I had ever had—ever hoped for—ay,
existence itself, to save that dear life. What did

it signify that mine was a hopeless love : hopeless
beyond redemption; bankrupt in even the power of
ever expressing itself, of ever coming to the knowledge of its object ; of being received with aught but
cruel scorn if it had done so ? Did that make it
more endurable ? Did that still one pulse of its
throbbings; quench one of the yearnings in which
my nature now asserted itself ? Oh ! Charles,
Charles !

But I would not waste the precious moments
thus. I must act, and without delay : return to
England by the most rapid conveyance that money
could secure. How I loathed myself now for this
fatal Swiss journey : for that scarcely avowed
suggestion of my own heart that, until something
was decided, the further I could be removed from the
scene the better. A murderous thought, an accursed
thought ! Wickedly conceived, and wickedly acted
upon ! And here was the result !

But for that false step, there would have been no
risk now. Wholly unexpected by me as this new
turn of matters had been, it would have been of no
moment, hardly, had I been nearer : I could at once
have come forward, produced the unhappy proofs,

assigned the bloodshed, to its real although guiltless perpetrator. But now, but now! Why, it would be days before I could reach England; before any communication from me could be received there :—*It might be too late!*

Oh! Heaven, let me start this very hour! Send a courier, an express? No indeed. They did not love : their speed would not be mine. Alone ; unprotected? Oh! yes, everything. Let me start.

CHAPTER V.

I DID not pause to look at the *Galignani*. I had an intuitive certainty that the speaker in the church-yard had quoted the paragraph there correctly; why waste time upon it?

I did not pause for that or for anything; excepting to place together in a travelling-bag the merest necessaries, and to give directions at the hotel in regard to Mr. Fortescue. With the latter I decided not to communicate before leaving. His health was so greatly restored that he required little special attendance, and the proprietor, on my mentioning that I was recalled to England by urgent business, readily undertook that this should be forthcoming. Of money there was fortunately an ample supply in hand. I took from this what I required, and then stepped into the travelling-carriage which was already

at the door. Safely secured about me were Fred's
cross, and the fatal implement with which his death
had been effected:—objects of terrible association in
themselves, but dear to me as the jewels of Paradise;
for were they not Charles' salvation? I would have
parted with hand and eye sooner than have had them
torn from me!

Our journey to the Münster Thal had been a
slow one, for there was an invalid's health in charge.
My return from it was urged with the utmost speed
that money could purchase; for there was life and
death in the result!

But, urge it as I would, it was pitiably tardy:
seemingly interminable.

Back at Basle at last; but not until long after
midnight. The whole afternoon lost in a vexatious
break-down on the road; patched up, half-a-dozen
times over, by expedients which carried us on a mile
or two, and then broke down again.

Back at Basle. And then confronted by that
dreary journey across the whole main continent of
Europe. There were no railroads then; not even
the Rhine steamers which preceded them. Nothing
for it, but to plod on to Paris: to plod on from

Paris to the coast. Days and nights: days and nights!

Back at Basle; through Basle; out of Basle. All full of annoyances; routine difficulty; gnawing to the heart of this fraction of time that was so priceless! Still in the Rhine valley, when the April morning broke over it, tearful with rain and then bright with golden sunshine; streaming on the reaches of the fair river, the green crops and bursting foliage of its valley; the mountain outline swelling gracefully on its horizon. I turned my head away from those hills: I could not bear to look at them. They lay between me and Paris!

In our journey out we had taken the circuitous route by Strasbourg. But I did not follow this now; I took one quite unknown to me. Thann, Epinal, Mirecourt; such were the posting names I heard: entire strangers. Immaterial what route. Only let it be the straightest and shortest!

Two whole days from Basle, and two whole nights;—then, the end of the third day would bring me into Paris.

How those first forty-eight hours passed, I have no knowledge. I changed the carriage; ate and drank,

or sat down to food; looked, heard, spoke : all in
an utter dream. I could not have identified one
person, one object afterwards. Confused images of
ascent and descent. Of the road painfully toiling
upwards among woods; stretching intolerably in
advance, league after league, over the billowy table-
land; dipping into cool green valleys, where the water
flowed. Of the noisy shouts and *sacres* of the
postilions in their blouses ;—as little heeded by the
horses as the tantalizing crack of the whip, incessantly in action, but never employed to extract one
mile of speed out of the wretched teams. Of the
field-labourers looking up from their work as we
passed, saluting the driver with a nod of recognition,
or gazing curiously at the solitary passenger. Of the
acres of dusty vineyard, the gaunt poplars, the dreary
arable lands, studded with no trim cottages as in
England, but huddling all their life into the nearest
town or village. Of the sun streaming in at the
right window of the carriage all the forenoon, and
then shifting round to the other side as the day
waned. Of the sense of relief when the shadows
began perceptibly to lengthen, and the churches rang
the " Angelus," and the peasants plodded home

wearifully from their work. Of nightfall; the
looming houses of the villages; the lights by cottage
hearths ; the women's hymn to Mary, the Mother-
Virgin ; the open road again, the blackness all round,
the sleep that would come and yet would not be
sleep. Images of all these ; but no connected idea :
no apprehension even, beyond what was surface-
deep :—cold reflections as from a mirror, while the
soul within still brooded unchangeably over its one
thought !

This was the forty-eight hours. And then at
Chalons-sur-Marne, the third day broke ; and the
third night, as I have said, would fall in Paris.
I remembered the road now. We had joined the
main route which Mr. Fortescue and myself had
followed to Strasbourg ; the objects began to be
familiar : I recollected Chalons ; its beautiful bridge ;
its stately cathedral ; the crowding spires of its
churches and dismantled convents. But I recollected
as I saw and heard ;—still in a dream : the memory
acted, but the mind received no impression from it.
All blank there : all but that, its one thought ;—
could I be in time ? Thus far all had been well
since leaving Basle : as well as the circumstances

admitted ; no recurrence of accident ; no delays but what had been inevitable. But still slow : very slow. *Could* I be in time ?

The day over at last ; the rich Marne valley falling into that of the Seine. Paris !

Light enough still to distinguish the high ground of Montmartre as we approached ; the two towers of Notre Dame ; the Tuileries. One pang shot across my mind as I contrasted my bright honeymoon there, so few weeks since, with the dark present : and yet hardly a pang ; it disappeared almost before felt. My heart was bleeding in every vein : there was no room for any fresh wound.

I began to feel deadly tired. My head throbbed almost to bursting with the sleepless nights, the eternal clatter of the wheels ; it craved a brief interval : some hours' cessation and repose. But I would not hear of it. What ! Rest, refresh myself while that issue was at stake ! There was one rest, and one only :—to reach England.

My two trips abroad had taught me something of travelling, and I drove at once to the bureau of the Malle-post for Calais, as that would be much faster than any other conveyance. Alas ! all the

places engaged; but the diligence, they kindly told
me, would soon start, and usually caught the same
packet as the mail : Madame could probably obtain a
seat by that at the Messageries.

No, I did not dare: I could not chance it.
Usually, the clerk said; but not always: certainly
not always. Doubtless if Madame wanted to make
sure of the packet, it would be the preferable thing
that she should post.

A choking duty meal; and then out on the road
again. But this night I was overborne with sleep,
and was conscious of little.

Conscious of nothing, in fact, until I was roused
by a vehement altercation outside the carriage. I
feared at first that some accident had occurred
similar to that in the Münster Thal ; but I soon
discovered that this, at any rate, was not the case.
We were drawn up in the courtyard of an hotel ;—
apparently, from the meanness of its buildings and
appointments, the inn of some country village only.
It was just daybreak ; and the fresh field-scented air
which the dawn brought with it, confirmed me in
this idea. But why were we stopping here ? I could
discover nothing amiss with the vehicle itself; but

there were no horses put to, nor any to be seen about
the inn-yard.

I listened to the angry parley going on near me,
and soon ascertained what had happened. One of
the speakers was the postilion who had driven me
the last stage ; the other appeared to be the proprietor of the inn, a rough, country-built man, who
was defending himself warmly against the abuse
lavished upon him by my driver. Between the two,
my chance of horses for the next stage had fallen to
the ground. My late driver had, as he believed,
arranged satisfactorily for them on his arrival, and
had then gone indoors to get an early cup of coffee ;
meanwhile the diligence from Paris had come up—
having overtaken me during the night; and, having a
heavy load, had taken on the horses which had been
ordered for myself, and was already some way with
them on its road. They were the only horses in the
village !

The proprietor was endeavouring to excuse himself for his breach of faith as he best might. "He
had not been aware that Madame was so pressed :
there were other horses he could send for from the
farm of a cousin of his own ; they were much better

horses, and would take Madame forward excellently : if she would only repose herself for two or three hours while they were being fetched. Perhaps Madame would breakfast before she started."

I saw through the device, and could have cursed the paltry artifice which risked a life ; but it was useless exhibiting any resentment. Cutting short the altercation, I assured the landlord that it was impossible I should alight : he should send me coffee where I sat ; it was the only breakfast I could take, and he was most welcome to charge for it as such. But he and the driver must arrange for my going forward : I must have the old horses.

Impossible. It was strictly prohibited by the regulations. And they could not do it, poor animals : the next stage was hilly, wretched road ; that was why the diligence had required assistance : and they had come far, too, the last stage.

It required the promise of a Napoleon apiece to overcome these difficulties ; but I succeeded with this aid. How cheaply spent the dross seemed !

The horses, who certainly looked jaded enough, were brought out of the stable and put to : we started at last. But oh ! the time that had been squandered! The time that was still lost, mile after mile, in this lamentable "next stage!" The road was wretched enough, as the landlord had said: trying even for fresh animals; and ours were beat before they started!

How wearily I held my watch in my hand, trying to gauge our pace by some computation of that at which I had previously travelled! How tired I got of this; how I then sat, straining in the early sunrise for the glimpse of some church-spire or mill, which might indicate our approach to the town where the stage was to terminate! How I hated myself for having allowed my senses to desert me at that critical time! Why had I not watched, and then the trick would not have been played? What had I to do with sleep any more?

Over at last. Sooner than I had once or twice dared to hope: sooner then it would have been, but for the incessant exertions of my postilion, who, ashamed probably of his previous negligence, and seeing my intense anxiety to proceed, did all in his power to urge the horses forward. A little sooner, a little better, in these respects; but oh! how cruelly late to what it should have been! "The diligence,"

I inquired passionately, the moment we stopped at the door of an hotel.

"The diligence? Oh! but it had departed, Madame."

"Yes, yes. But how long ago?"

Alas! An hour: an hour and a half: between one and two hours. And the diligence itself did not always catch the packet: only usually!

Forward again. Good horses now; no drawback. Everything well appointed,—as foreign appointments went,—all the way. But the diligence still keeping before us: well ahead.

It was a race between us all day: all that day and through the night. I clung to the pursuit with the energy of desperation, for I knew it was my last chance. If I were not at Calais before the diligence, I might as well not be there at all: the packet would be certainly gone. Constantly we seemed nearing the object of our chase. Always hearing of it at the towns and villages as " only just left:" " scarcely up the hill yet." Always straining eye and ear in quest of it; expecting while light lasted, to see it on the next ridge of road, in the dip of the next hollow. Expecting, all night long, to hear its

jangling harness just in advance, before us.   Always
expecting, and always disappointed !

During the final stages, however, the race slackened ;
our distance from the vehicle was evidently increasing :
I gave up inquiring for it.

And then at last we neared Calais.   It was
already day; and a slight rise in the road enabled
me to see the harbour and sea beyond : Dover cliffs
were plainly visible.   And, standing over towards
them in the fair morning light, half-an-hour or so
outside the Calais piers, and with all sail set, was the
packet which I had been straining every nerve to
reach !   Had I kept to the diligence, I found, I
should have been in ample time.

No packet till the following morning at the same
hour.   Another twenty-four hours struck off the fast
lessening sum !   For twenty-four hours, bound hand
and foot, in this wretched port, with my whole
heart yearning for the unapproachable white cliffs
opposite !

It was intolerable : I must engage a boat myself
and cross at all hazards.   The morning had already
clouded over, and it threatened to blow hard ; but I
was not to be deterred by that : I hurried to the

quay, and endeavoured to find something that would take me over.

Alas! baffled: beat at all points. None of the fishing-smacks were going out that day; and the owners of the boats in the harbour positively refused to risk the passage in such weather. One of the larger craft might have gone, possibly; but on inquiring the price of this; I found that it was hopelessly beyond my means. I had provided myself for an ordinary journey; but the expenses of this had been heavy, and the money I had left would do little more than pay the common packet-fare to Dover, with a balance for the necessary posting beyond. I must wait, perforce. Oh! agony!

As the day wore on, I became more contented that I had not started. The gale had now increased to a storm, the wind howling, with torrents of rain; and no ordinary boat could have lived it out in the Channel. For my miserable self this would have signified but little, I felt: a grave under those foaming seas might have been no hard lot. I was heart-broken: what mattered it to me now how soon the end came? But for *him*: that was what I had to look to. Jealously and carefully must I guard my

life for his sake, until my mission was completed. I
almost regretted now that I had kept myself as the
sole depositary of the secret on which that dear life
hung. But I was nearing the goal at last, and it
was not probable that any accident would intervene.

And so the twenty-four hours passed; listening
to that upbraiding wind, that desolating rain: seeking no amusement; no occupation. Amusement!
occupation! The thought was blasphemy. Sitting
on, thinking, thinking. Not thinking of my own
heavy guilt in the sight of God and man. No. The
time for that had not come yet:—it was there;
looming before me, that dark terror, but it had not
stepped palpably forward as yet. Not even thinking
now, of *his* peril; of the consequences that would
ensue if all my haste, all my exertions should prove
nugatory: if I should be too late, after all! That
fear too was present to me : present enough, as it
had been throughout this weary journey. But I did
not think about it. I thought of one thing only :
of *him*.

Every word he had ever spoken to me, spoken in
my hearing; his step outside our schoolroom; his
voice in the garden; every look of his, every

lineament, every movement ; trivial incidents, matters that no human being could have recalled as express memories, all crowded upon me, all at once ; just as they say the detail of a drowning man's life comes back upon him. Where they had been treasured up all these months : what page in my heart, unconsciously to myself, had kept this transcript, so minute and exact, yet so fatally concealed, I knew not—I did' not seek to know. I knew one thing ; that these memories of an outraged love, which I could not shun, which I would not have shunned if I could, were writing themselves plainly enough now : burning into soul and brain like fire !

CHAPTER VI.

AGAIN the packet standing out between those two piers of Calais. And I was aboard this time. Thank Heaven for that, at least.

The wind had entirely gone down during the night, and the April morning was calm and beautiful, although cold. I had placed myself in the forepart of the boat : it seemed nearer to England. And I could there too see uninterruptedly those buttresses of white cliff which to me were like the thrones of Seraphim. Oh! once to set my foot upon them!

A cold morning, and I was lightly clad; I felt instinctively in my travelling bag for something to tie round my throat. As I took out what I had been in quest of, a small book fell out with it : my memorandum-book, as I soon saw. I had not used it for some weeks, and had forgotten it was there. It had fallen open at the fly-leaf; and as I took it up to replace it, my eye was caught by some pencil-writing on the leaf, in my own hand. I read thus :—"11th October 18 . . . See what Mr. Charles Armitage thinks of his dream this day six months."

Six months? Eleventh of October? That would be the eleventh of April. I turned to the steward, who happened to be standing near.

" What day of the month is it, if you please," I asked : " I have been travelling so rapidly that I have got confused."

"No wonder, Ma'am," said the man, touching his hat ; " going about among those Mounseers too. But it's the eleventh to-day; and a beautiful morning it is : quite a change from yesterday."

I muttered some thanks, and sat down, trembling violently. Well I recollected that conversation on the esplanade at Hastings, when Charles told me of the dream in the boat which had impressed him so strangely : impressed him with that presage of death. Every word, every inflection of his voice, rung in my ear as if he was still speaking. But I had forgotten this act of my own : this entry in the pocket-book. Good Heaven! what

did the coincidence mean ?   Was this further omen
needed ?

No, it should not be an omen.

As we sped along with a fair wind and all sail
set, nearing the English coast perceptibly every half-
hour, something of my old stout heart and strong
will came back to me : my depression lightened, in
spite of the past.   No, I would not accept this, or
any other augury ; my toil, my endurance should not
be in vain : Charles should be saved.   Must there
not be time ?   Why, of course yes !   How needlessly
had I been tormenting myself!   Even supposing
. . . . . supposing the worst ; supposing the trial
over, and a verdict of guilty given, nothing could
be done at once : for some days at least.   It could
not possibly be.   Strange that I should not have
thought of this !   Ample time, of course !   Charles
was safe, safe !

The thought gave a new impulse to my whole
system.   My own wretchedness, the guilty past, the
hopeless future, all were forgotten : I thought only
of him, and my heart bounded with exultation.   I
could see the blue water sparkling now, the smile
of the spring sky, the bright faces round me, re-

turning to home and love. I was not returning
to home and love :—oh! Heaven, no. But I was
as gay as they were ;—much gayer. The intolerable
fear was removed ; the phantom laid : Charles
was safe !

So, when at last we touched the quay at Dover :
so, when after a hurried meal, I stepped into the
post-chaise at the Ship door ; climbed the white
ascent by Shakspeare's cliff; felt the exhilarating
speed of the English horses, and sped, rapidly and
prosperously, along the well-kept roads and under the
trim hedgerows of the Kentish coast.

Still more so, when Kent changed to Sussex, and
I reached places which I could connect by name with
my Hastings life. The direct route to Lewes lay
through that town ; and at first I was distressed at
this, and would, if possible, have avoided it. But in
my present mood, the approach to these familiar
scenes gave me a feeling of added hope : Charles
used to talk about these places. In my recollection,
they belonged to him : they were old friends, assuring
me of his well-being, his security. Dungeness Point.
He had been becalmed off that once for several hours
in a boat, and nearly drifted out by the current.

Rye. Charles had a friend there whom he occasionally sailed over to see; an old cockswain, who had been at the Nile and Trafalgar, and now tenanted a cabin adjoining the south wall of the town, where he employed himself in the cultivation of a vine of fabulous dimensions. Cumber Castle, on the flat beyond Rye. Charles used to go shooting gulls there. Winchelsea. That was where the Olivers lived; and Helen used to fancy Charles liked the eldest Miss Oliver. Pett, Fairlight; the range of our school-walks now:—he often walked bits of the way with us; or we met him out shooting or riding. Then the Castle,—Hastings Castle:—Hastings itself. Ah! but I could not look at *that;* I feared that might have some menace about it: every turn in the winding homely street, every stone in its pavement, was instinct with him; might cry out against me, who had so nearly, so nearly, done to death what I loved so passionately. So nearly been *his* murderer! So I leant back as far as I could in the carriage, hiding my face in the cushions. It was well perhaps that I did so, as it prevented my being recognized. Not that I had any thought of that. I thought of nothing but him: nothing.

At the hotel we stopped to change horses, and I was obliged to speak to the landlady; a kind-hearted, compassionate soul. She looked inquisitively at me; although, as I could see, without knowing who I was. But she pressed me earnestly, unless my journey was of paramount haste, to alight for a few hours and have some sleep and refreshment. "If you will excuse my saying it, Ma'am," she said, "you look as if you wanted some one to take care of you: you have been in terrible trouble, I can see that; and if you go on, you will break down, and that before very long, too. If the money is any object," continued the good soul, with some hesitation, and, doubtless, drawing her conclusions from my travel-soiled exterior, "do not think about that. There is our little sitting-room upstairs; or you can lie down on my daughter's bed, and I can send you up something when we dine ourselves: it's not far from one o'clock."

I thanked the landlady cordially for her kindness, assuring her how gratefully I would have accepted it, had my circumstances been what she supposed. But I must press forward with all speed, I said: my business was most urgent.

The post-chaise for the next stage was ready in a few minutes. I stepped into it, and for the second time said farewell to Hastings. I quitted the town this time, not by the Battle road, but still keeping along the coast ; — by the Martello towers and Bexhill. The road was sandy, and the pace was very slow at times; far different from what it had been from Dover : the exhilarating motion was gone, and my spirits began to sink in proportion. The landlady's kindness too had touched me deeply : my mind was just in the excited state when it vibrated powerfully to any impulse of the kind; and I was weak too, pitiably weak; exhausted with my long journey, with the prolonged agitation and suspense of these terrible days. I burst into tears ; sobbed passionately.

Ah ! but this would not do : I should become hysterical; fall ill ; be prevented from finishing my task. There were only two or three hours more ; but I might break down even in this time. "Before very long," the landlady had said; and I felt she was right. I would husband, for his sake, every grain of strength; avoid all excited feeling, force myself into calmness, until my errand was sped :—and then, come what would. The speedier and more complete the end might then be, the better!

I checked my sobs, dried away every vestige of tears, and forced myself to look out on surrounding objects; to try and recall the hopeful feelings of the forenoon.

But I could not succeed. The emotion aroused by the passing sympathy of a stranger still throbbed at my heart, tinging everything with a subdued and saddened hue. There was the blue sea sparkling on my left all the way; the pleasant fields, the farms and villages. But the shadow had begun to fall upon them all once more : that old foreboding of the Münster Thal — that which had haunted me there, even before I heard the voices in the churchyard!

Very slow our progress seemed. The horses were tired ;—had been out with parties the whole of the week, the driver told me, apologetically. "Was there no posting-house on the way, where we could change?" I asked. No, these must take us through to Lewes. There was no help for it.

Past Bexhill, with its pleasant headland. A further weary drag, and then the mouldering towers

and historic beach of Pevensey. Then, at last, East-
bourne on our left; a retired village, nestling under
the Downs, and little conscious of the repute and
fashion it was ultimately to attain ; and then we
first turned inland for Lewes. "Over you," the
driver said, as he pointed out a bold hill at some
miles' distance, joining the main line of the Beechy
Head range : "just under that hill."

The goal was then at last in sight ! Fortunate
that the speakers in the Münster Thal had mentioned
Lewes. I should not have known otherwise that the
assizes were now going on there ; should have been
compelled to ask questions and provoke inquiry in
return ; perhaps should have lost precious time by
a futile quest for Charles at Hastings. As it was,
I knew that he must be in the town which we were
now approaching.

Approaching. But how slowly ; how dispro-
portionately to the cruel terror which had now once
more settled down upon me ! Without cause, no
doubt. I could assign no sufficient ground for it ;
could suggest, as I had done in the morning, twenty
reasons why I need not entertain it. But I could
not *feel* them. Every mile the foreboding deepened

upon me: that foreboding of something, I knew not what.

The sun was sinking upon Beechy Head, and the steep chalk-ridge of which it forms the termination already threw a long and sombre shadow over the marshes traversed by the road. I shuddered as an unexpected turn brought us within it. "The shadow of the valley of death." That was the phrase Charles had used when telling me of his dream in the boat: and here was the shadow. Was it indeed to be the "valley of death" which stretched beneath it?— The words rung in my ear like the strokes of a passing-bell.

"Lewes 1 mile." We had joined a main road, and this milestone came in sight immediately afterwards.

The main road; and at the present time a sufficiently crowded and busy one. Numerous vehicles, interspersed here and there with foot-passengers, were on their way back from the town; doubtless after the termination of the day's ordinary assize business. And yet there was something in their manner which arrested my attention too; the different knots of drivers and walkers were conversing, in many instances gesticulating, with an eagerness

which seemed hardly to be accounted for by any
business of the courts, however interesting : their
manner was more that of persons who have just
witnessed some exciting and painful scene, and are
occupied ·in discussing its details. I grew intensely
terrified. What had happened ? Should I stop
and ask ?

No ; no. On.

Just outside the town, among the straggling
buildings of its suburb, we were met by a party of a
different character ;—a small body of mounted soldiers :
they were riding out of the town at a smart trot.
The occupants of the houses on each side were
grouped at the doors, looking at them in silence, and
with an undefined expression of curiosity; as if something unusual had been going on. I could bear it no
longer, and begged the driver, who was ready enough
to do so, to pull up and ascertain what had occurred.
But this was no longer possible. The street was now
crowded with knots of eager talkers, who had made
way temporarily for the passage of the soldiers, and
then returned to their discussion ; making the horses
restive with the confusion, and requiring all the man's
attention to get through them.

As we entered the main street, the crowd and bustle increased with every hundred yards, culminating in front of the inn at which I was to alight, and which seemed to form the focus of the excitement. It was with the utmost difficulty that room was made for the carriage to drive up to the door. The proprietor, as he seemed to be, was standing there with several gentlemen, all talking earnestly; he at once came forward and spoke to me, civilly enough. "He greatly regretted the inconvenience to which I had been subjected, and still more so, as he feared he could not accommodate me. But perhaps I was intending to post forward; if so, he would endeavour. . . ."

"No, no," I cried, stopping him short. I had husbanded my whole remaining strength for this moment; but it proved little enough: I could say nothing coherent; could hardly speak at all, excepting in a kind of hoarse whisper. "No, no," I cried; "not that. Him; him! Is it going on? is he safe?"

Seeing my agitation, one of the gentlemen by the door stepped forward to the side of the carriage; a grave-looking, middle-aged man. "Can I be of any service to you," he said, taking off his hat, and bowing courteously. "You were inquiring for some one."

"Yes," I said, "oh yes. Save him, save him! I have the evidence. He is innocent—wholly innocent."

"Of whom do you speak?" the gentleman asked. "The prisoner, young Armitage?"

"Yes: of whom else should I? Save him, for the love of Heaven, or help me to do it. I have everything, all the . . . . You shall not say it," I broke off with a passionate cry, almost a shout, seeing that my companion hesitated; "you shall not: the trial is not over; it is not too late!"

"No," he answered gently: "the trial is not over; but——"

The speaker did not complete his sentence. My powers had been overtasked, and now gave way utterly. A deadly chill; a rush of blood to the head, as if every vein in my body had emptied itself there; and then I fell back into the carriage, out of which I had partly stepped. I felt myself at once propped by kind and careful arms; borne into the entrance-hall; supported on a chair. I was vaguely conscious of persons speaking in whispers near me; caught two or three of the sentences. "A singular complication in the matter, and wholly unexpected." "Beautiful young creature too: who can she be?" "Seems about his own age." "Really a terrible business altogether: a terrible business."

Then hearing deserted me, and I sank down in the death of swoon, motionless and senseless.

CHAPTER VII.

My story must now for a short space be a retrospect, commencing with the period which followed Helen Armitage's examination and committal, some two or three weeks before the events described in the last chapter. That fatal period! In which so many circumstances had concurred, so simply, and yet with such disastrous result!

As before, this part of my narrative is derived from many different sources, embracing particulars which in some instances came to my knowledge soon after they occurred, but in many others not until the lapse of several years. As before also, let me write them, not in the desultory mode in which I thus became acquainted with them, but as they now form a connected whole in my memory.

The circumstances connected with Helen Armi-

tage's committal have been detailed in the preceding
volume. Bail having been accepted for her as there
mentioned, it was arranged that she should remain
at Harcourt Villa for the short interval which must
elapse before it would be necessary for her to be
removed to Lewes for trial. Mrs. Armitage made a
show of offering this accommodation with a suppression of all resentful feeling towards Helen, and a
determination to believe in her innocence as long as
possible. " Of course," she said, " under these
highly painful circumstances it would be impossible
for her to have any personal communication with
Miss Armitage. But she was perfectly willing to offer
her the protection of her roof meanwhile, and trusted
the event would show that she might still continue to
do so." So Helen occupied her own room at the Villa
as before, with the small upstairs sitting-room on the
same floor.

It was here that Mr. Latrobe found her on the
morning following the examination. He had been
intolerably anxious for a private interview with Helen
the afternoon before, but she was so evidently
exhausted with her appearance before the magistrates that he was compelled to forbear. This

morning he hastened to the Villa at the earliest
hour he could hope to find her out of her room.

" I am so glad you can see me," he said on entering. " I do so long for a few earnest words with you
about this matter, if only you are equal to it. I feared
so much what yesterday might do."

Helen was standing by the fire-place, her arm
leaning on the mantelpiece and supporting her face.
She turned when the curate spoke. The poor girl had
borne up stoutly hitherto, but the kind voice and
words were now too much for her : she hid her face
again in her hands, sobbing. " Oh! Mr. Latrobe,
she said, " why do you come here ? How can you
speak to me, or think of me, with all this shame
upon me ? I ought not to allow it, for your own
sake."

Hyacinthe Jean was as good as gold ; but he was
human. Down the winds went vows and resolutions.
Over the salt waves fled the purposes of self-abne-
gating love, of a devotion in which its object should
recognize nothing but a friendly solicitude for her
welfare. He flung himself on a couch by the fire-
place, and taking Helen's disengaged hand, pressed
it to his lips long and passionately. "Miss Armitage,

Helen," he cried; "I cannot bear this. Shame!
Shame upon *you*, of all created beings! Oh! Helen,
Helen, my heart's darling, give me but the right to
share that shame—to link it with my name, with my
life—and see what my joy and gratitude will be!
Helen, dearest, I did not mean to speak of this: you
know I did not; but the words would come. And
yet I am a brute to go on. Miss Armitage, forgive
me if you can: I will never offend again. Say you
forgive me, Miss Armitage!"

Helen hid her face, still sobbing. But a crimson
flush overspread the part of the cheek which was
visible, passing down to the exquisitely fair neck.
Then she said, very low and gently, "There are not
many people to call me Helen now. You may do so,
if you think it worth while."

"Helen! My own, own Helen! Life of my
life, love of my love! Helen! Always Helen
now!"

The words leapt from the speaker with a cry
almost of agony, such as intense joy alone can utter.
To fold in his arms the scarcely resisting girlish form
before him; to imprint one deep, deep kiss upon the
lips, was a moment's work:—one of those moments

measured by no time, crowding centuries and ages into their passage, teaching even man's dull heart that love, like its Author, is infinite!

Then, a very, very long interval, with which Helen's consent had little enough to do. She at last succeeded in disengaging herself, and spoke again: but not sobbing now. "The shame *is* upon me, notwithstanding," she said—"as far, that is, as it can be on one wholly and entirely innocent. Were it not for that indeed I would not have let you come here to-day, however it might have wrung your kind heart. Would certainly not have let you . . . say what you have. And now, I can only listen to it conditionally. Until this disgrace, wrongful as it is, is completely removed from me, I cannot allow you to be more to me than—than the kind friend you always have been."

"You require my consent to that now, dearest," said the curate. "However," he continued, "it was about this matter that I paid you the visit which has turned out so happily for myself. Not the disgrace, as you call it, but about your position altogether. I came here to-day to implore you, by every persuasion in my power, to clear up the mystery connected with your movements on that unhappy evening. What frightened you ? What prevented your going back to your own room ? Helen, love, you will surely tell me now ?"

Helen hesitated for a minute, while a deep flush, deeper even than that which had lately been there, again overspread her face and neck. " I cannot," she said at last : " I cannot tell it, even to you. Do not think me obstinate, ungrateful for your kindness," she added. " It is not that. But I could not bear to speak of it ; cannot think of it even ; it was so painful, so agitating : such an overpowering shock. And then, with that poor child's loss, happening just at the same time ! I cannot understand it : cannot guess what it all means. It was my thinking about it, and trying to find some clue to the mystery, which, with the strangeness and terror of the thing itself, brought on my illness. Indeed, indeed, if you love me as you say you do——"

" Helen ! " ejaculated the curate.

" Well then, if you love me, indeed, indeed, you will not urge me further. I promise you this much," continued Helen, " that if any actual necessity should arise, I will give you, or others, the explanation you

wish. I do not myself see how there can be any such
necessity ; for although the circumstances look suspicious, and the magistrates were probably right in
sending the case for trial at the assizes in consequence, still this is no proof of guilt. However, I
promise you that if there should then be any risk of
. . . of an unfavourable verdict there, I will tell
everything. Even then I might not be believed.
I told Mr. Sims in confidence, and I could see that
he disbelieved me ; and so might others :—that is
another reason why I shrink from mentioning it
unless absolutely compelled. So please, please do
not urge it further. There is a horror to me about
the whole thing."

Mr. Latrobe was dissatisfied, but saw no alternative excepting to leave the matter as it was. He
feared too, from the undoubted influence which the
circumstance, whatever it was, had had in causing
Helen's illness, that if she were unduly pressed upon
the subject her health, so recently restored, might
suffer in consequence. Meanwhile, he had Helen's
promise that the mystery should be cleared up,
if necessary for her safety ; and he also knew
that in the ultimate resort, he had other means of

insuring this, however painful it might be to use them.

So Mr. Latrobe returned to his bachelor lodgings with a lighter heart than he had ever before brought there. He could have wished, on all accounts, that the dark cloud which at present rested over Helen, might have been dispersed ; as he had no doubt it at once would be, by her statement of the circumstances which at present appeared so difficult to account for. In his present frame of mind however the curate was not disposed to consider the absence of this satisfaction any serious hardship ; still less to anticipate disaster of any kind from his failure in the primary object of his recent visit to Harcourt Villa.

CHAPTER VIII.

A few days after the conversation between Mr. Latrobe and Helen which had proved so auspicious to the hopes of the former, Charles Armitage paid a visit to the fisherman Ralph and his wife at their cottage. It was the first time he had been out since Helen's examination, and now he carefully avoided the streets of the town; leaving the Villa by a back gate which opened on the hill above, and then skirting under the latter until he reached the fishermen's houses on the beach.

Ralph was at home, and shook hands with Charles with his usual heartiness; although, as his visitor fancied, with some embarrassment of manner.

"Ye're right welcome, sir," he said; "now and allus. We haven't seed you here this month and more."

"I hadn't the heart to come, old boy," said Charles. "I'm hard hit: very hard hit. I can't bear it much longer, I think."

Ralph looked at him with a curious expression of scrutiny in his eye. "You're meaning that about the . . . about what the young lady was had up for the other day, sir?" he asked.

"Yes, Ralph. But you must ask me nothing about it please. I did not mean to have spoken then, but the words would come. You're the only friend I have left now, Ralph, I think; they're all cutting me: even Mr. Latrobe; although I certainly did not expect it of him. However, I don't mind that, or anything else about myself: it's her trouble, Ralph.—It's killing me."

The fisherman again looked up at the speaker with the same singular expression;—respectful but inquisitive. "You see, Mr. Armitage," he said, after a pause, "it's a cruel business: a cruel piece of work, whoever dooed it; which I'd never believe it was the young lady. How was it likely?"

"It's no good, old boy," said Charles. "I mustn't talk about it: I can't; although my heart is breaking for not doing so. But I can't, even to you. I can't talk or think about anything, that's the fact: the power seems quite gone. Did you ever have the sort of feeling, Ralph, as if you were no use to anybody? As if you had better just lie down and let the first fellow that likes come and knock you on the head?"

"I don't know, sir," said Ralph. "I don't think I should ever feel like that: not unless I'd been and dooed something to make people ashamed of me. I should be like enough to knock myself on the head then, I fancy."

"I didn't mean that sort of thing, Ralph," said Charles. "I meant being of no use to other people. Having somebody that you loved very much, for instance, who was in great trouble, and yet do what you would, you couldn't help them: couldn't stir a finger. Could do nothing but just look on like an idiot."

"I do know that, sir," said Ralph. "I'd a little sister who died, just when she were twelve yearn old. She went off in something, I don't mind the name the doctors gave it; but it was a sort of wasting away. All the food she took wouldn't nourish her, and at last it were no good giving her even that: she couldn't swallow it. She just lay the last two or three days, with us looking at her; no more use, as you say, sir, than babbies: and yet, I'd have de'ed to save her. Poor little Jessie; with them blue, blue eyes of her'n, that allus seemed as if they were looking for something that weren't in this world! I couldn't bide with her at last; it broke my heart to. Nor I can't think of her now, though it's ever so many yearn sin'. But be ye going, sir?"

"Yes, Ralph," said Charles. "I'm poor company for you or any one else, now. How's the tide?"

"Turned, sir, this hour or two."

"Then I can get along under the cliffs: there'll be no one there. Good-by, old boy. Good-by, Mrs. Ralph."

The fisherman looked after his visitor as he left the cottage, slowly taking his way in the direction of the beach under the East cliff;—the same where I had walked myself on the occasion which nearly terminated so disastrously.

"He don't seem to know the least what they're a-talking of about himself," said Ralph.

"Do you think he don't?" asked the wife.

"I'm quite sure on't," said Ralph. "And I'm

not going to be the one as shall tell him, poor lad.
It's singular like, too, that he should not have
heard something: to-day, at any rate, if he hadn't
before."   ·

" What's doing to-day then, Ralph?" the wife
again asked.

" I don't know as anything will come of it,"
the fisherman answered; "most like not: least-
ways, nothing to the lad's harm. I'd sooner cut
my hand off than think he had aught to do with that
business. It's only a further search they're making
of," continued Ralph, stopping the question which
his wife was about to repeat. " I heerd it as I came
through the town just now."

" Search, Ralph! What for? Where?"

" There," answered the fisherman, pointing with
his thumb towards the Castle Hill. "Where it
was found, you know. And I'll tell you what it
is, Missus; I'll just go up there and see what's
a-doing: they must have been at it some hours
now."

" Ye'll have yere dinner first, Ralph?"

" No, mother, I don't feel as if I could get it
down to-day: it would choke me. I've a notion

there's something up; though I don't guess what it is, or why I think so : but I can't rest without seeing."

The wife would have pressed further questions, but Ralph took his weather-beaten glazed hat and departed.

Charles meanwhile had been slowly pursuing his way under the cliffs in the direction he had indicated.

He found this walk as retired as he had hoped. The tide was just out; and even at any time, as I had experienced in my own case, the two miles of shingle and weedy rock between Hastings and the preventive station were rarely traversed either by inhabitants or visitors. Charles followed it for about half the distance, and then flung himself on the beach, by some broken masses of the cliff.

It was a bright day, and he looked out at the sea, studded with fishing-craft, and tracked in the offing by numerous homeward-bound vessels, which stood along with a fair breeze for the Downs. Charles tried to interest himself in the animated scene before him.

"Just the day for a sail," he said. "Whose is

that yacht, I wonder, coming round the corner now? Oh! I know, Petric's. He can't be sailing her himself, though, for he's abroad. A sail and a bathe too, to-day; it's quite warm enough. But there's no getting a boat without going through the town, and that I *can't* do. And it wouldn't be much use either; it wouldn't bring the old times back again. I think it's worse for a fellow," Charles continued, musingly, and speaking half aloud, "it's worse for him going and doing things as he used, when it's all really changed. He can't force the thoughts out of his head as if he were a machine : they will come; and they come all the more when one is putting a sort of sham like that upon oneself. Why won't Latrobe see me? it's so awfully unlike what he used to be. He couldn't help us, of course ; I know that : nobody can, that I can see. But it would be something to talk it over with him ; and I've got nobody : nobody. It's so odd too ; people seem to whisper and point so, whenever I meet them. Old Ralph just now, even, seemed quite unlike what he usually is.

"Of course, I don't care," Charles continued in the same sort of half-spoken soliloquy, pausing in it now and then to throw a pebble into the receding waves. "I don't mind being cut, or whatever it is, for myself: I'm rather glad that some part of it should fall on me. I wish I could take it all, Leenie dear. Poor little Leenie; poor little Leenie: to think it should have come to this! And I *can't* help her: not one atom, really. I only do her harm, brute that I am! Of course, yes, I see it's much better I shouldn't talk to any one about it: I can't tell a lie, and say I believe her wholly innocent, when I don't. Innocent; yes, poor child: innocent enough really, in all conscience; but I can't say I don't believe it was her hand; so I only stutter and make a fool of myself, as I did when Ralph spoke about her just now; making matters ten times worse for her: as if there was any need of that.

"That's another thing too," Charles continued pursuing his train of thought, after a pause as before; "I can't say anything to comfort the poor girl herself: can't even talk to her about it. I don't dare to ask her where she was that night; what it was that happened. Ah! I can't think of it. Horrible! Of course, I've no fear of the present consequences. They'll understand all about it in court; there'll be some further proceedings, and then she'll be discharged: that'll be all right enough. But what an awful thing for her all her life afterwards! She doesn't seem to feel it herself: at least, she doesn't seem crushed with it; and I hope this will go on so. They say it does sometimes: people can't realise what they've said and done when they were delirious, and that sort of thing. But how awful to have this taint about her all her life:—actual blood upon her hands! And the way they will talk and shrug their shoulders everywhere! If they do it even to me, what will it be with herself! Poor Leonie; poor little darling!

"And it was all my fault, too," Charles burst out, after another pause in his soliloquy. "I ought to have stopped her giving her heart as she did to that villain Fortescue: that was the root of all the mischief. Of course I saw what was going on, but I thought it was all right; he seemed such an awfully jolly fellow. Scoundrel! I ought never to have let him be about the place without knowing more of him. And then to go and jilt her as he did! What a train of miseries all that has brought! But for that, she would never have got ill, and then nothing would

have happened. It's immensely rum, too: I can't
help thinking of that. As Latrobe said, how was it
possible she could do it all? Of all things in the
world about the most impossible, a fellow would have
said! And that was my fault, too," Charles went
on, his reflections taking a new turn : " all my fault.
What did I go and leave her alone for, as I did, just
to mope and make herself ill? Just like me to be
so selfish; thinking about poor Papa, and all the
rest of it, and not the least about her trouble! Leenie,
my poor dear; I can't cry for you, as I did at first:
I seem to have got past that somehow. But oh! I
would do anything, anything for you, if I only knew
how. If I could only take the blame myself! They
might swing me up fast enough, if it would only clear
you, poor darling! Best thing that could happen
to me, I expect."

Charles was here interrupted. While pursuing
the incoherent train of thought just described, his
eye had run over the beach and sea in front of him
without taking any distinct notice of what he was
thus looking at. His attention however was now
fixed by the appearance of a man—he could not at
first distinguish whom—making his way among the

broken rocks at no great distance. The man was approaching him, and evidently from his move-ments endeavouring to do so in such a manner as to avoid being seen by any one else ; skulking along under cover of the masses of fallen cliff, and not quitting one until he had ensured a similar shelter further on.

Some minutes were thus occupied ; Charles's eye following the stranger, whoever he was, closely and watchfully. At length the figure emerged from its concealment, and rapidly crossed a few yards of intervening shingle to Charles' side.

It was Ralph. There was an unusual sternness in his face which excited Charles' surprise almost as much as his sudden appearance on the spot. To explain both, it is necessary that the reader should be apprised of the circumstances to be detailed in the next chapter.

CHAPTER IX.

It is singular how simultaneously the same thought
often occurs to different minds.   Up to the time of
Helen Armitage's committal for trial, there were
probably not half-a-dozen persons in Hastings and
the neighbourhood who entertained a question that
she was in fact responsible for the actual commission
of the act with which she was charged, however its
moral culpability might be removed by the supposed
state of her mind at the time.   No sooner however
was she committed, than an immediate revulsion in
public feeling took place.   It seemed as if Mr.
Partridge's suggestion, in the conversation related a
few chapters back, as to the possibility of the guilt
really resting in another quarter, had been caught
up and echoed at once by scores of voices.   " The
brother." " Charles Armitage." " Young Armitage."

" Shouldn't wonder if he had something to do with
it." " Clear and direct motive." " Extraordinary
that people have not thought of this." Such were
the utterances which began to be freely circulated
through the town; the speaker usually overlooking
the fact that, up to the present moment, he had
himself shared in the obtuseness of perception which
he thus charged on other people.

These rumours were greatly aggravated by Charles
having kept to himself as he had lately done; rarely
venturing out of doors, and then, as to-day, choosing
the most unfrequented walks. As long as no imputation attached to himself, indeed, this fell in well
enough with the public ideas of what was right and
seemly on Helen's account; but directly suspicion
shifted in his own direction, Charles's obvious desire
to escape observation was interpreted by a wholly
different motive. It now seemed, more than anything, to favour the presumption of his being the
guilty party; or, at any rate, deeply implicated in
the crime which had been perpetrated. " Keeping
out of the way." " Afraid to show himself." " Quite
altered; something very wrong." " Will give them
the slip if they don't take care."

Gradually these rumours and surmises gathered to one distinct head :—the necessity of an immediate further investigation of the matter. The strength of the suspicions thus aroused, coupled with the absence, at present, of any confirmatory facts, naturally produced this result. " Could then no clue of any kind be discovered to the guilty party ? Was it certain that everything had been tried with this object: every avenue of search exhausted ?"

No : palpably not. At least, this became very palpable to the general mind, on the question being asked, and answered, by a new actor in the proceedings. One Mr. Phelps, a member of the London detective force.

At a dinner-party, a few days previously, the matter had been eagerly discussed in the presence of one of the local magistrates, and the employment of such a person suggested. The hint was acted upon ; and Mr. Phelps arrived by the mail, early in the morning of the day on which Charles paid Ralph the visit described in the last chapter. He was supplied with the depositions at the coroner's inquest, and those made on Helen's examination; all of which he carefully perused.

" Have you searched the place ? " was his first question, after completing his task.

" What place ? " said the Hastings superintendent.

" Where the child's body was found : what these deponents call the caverns."

" Oh ! yes, certainly : it was the first thing done."

" And you found nothing ? "

" Absolutely nothing. We cleared away a lot of the fallen earth and rubbish, but there was nothing to show for it."

" Cleared away a lot ! Do you mean that you did not remove the whole ? "

" No ; what would have been the use ? It was plain there was nothing there ; and it had cost ever so much shovelling away what we did. Besides, it wasn't safe : we should have brought the hill down upon us ; so we moved enough to satisfy ourselves, and left the rest."

" Then, if you ask me, Mr. Superintendent, I should say that you had not searched."

And when Mr. Phelps had thus answered his own question, it became clear to those present, and through them speedily to all Hastings, that "the caverns" had not been searched. And what had been thus left undone it was decided should be done that same forenoon.

When Ralph, after Charles' departure from the cottage, quitted his wife and went on his errand of inquiry to the Castle Hill, he found this work, of which he had heard some rumours in the morning, considerably advanced. The danger of executing it had not been exaggerated; but a large gang of labourers had been engaged, and the soil overhead, in which some ominous fissures already appeared, was hastily but securely shored up. The workmen then addressed themselves to the task of removing the fallen débris.

Almost their first discovery was the blocked passage leading to the cellar in communication with the curate's lodgings. They could not at first enter this passage, but its existence was made apparent by the subsidence of the upper portion of the fallen earth, leaving the aperture by which Mr. Latrobe had ascertained his position on his nocturnal visit. This success animated their exertions; and the mass of rubbish which alone interposed between this passage

and the spot where the body had been found, and
where the men were now working, began rapidly to
diminish: by the time that Ralph reached the spot
it was reduced nearly by a quarter. The passage
might now have been reached by clambering, but
Mr. Phelps gave strict orders that no one should
enter it until the business in hand was completed.
No special interest was in fact felt in it after the first
discovery, as it was surmised that it would only prove
to be one of the numerous windings of this singular
excavation : there were twenty similar ones all
round.

Several magistrates and other leading persons of
the town were now present; Mr. Latrobe among
them, devoured by the most cruel anxiety, which he
made a very unsuccessful effort at concealing; but
attention was so riveted on what was going on that
his disquietude attracted no notice. Through Mr.
Latrobe's assistance, Ralph, after some difficulty, got
admitted to the scene of operations, and stood in the
back-ground watching the removal of the earth.

Shovelful after shovelful ; load after load ;
barrow after barrow. The arch leading from the
blocked passage to the caverns was now almost

cleared; but Mr. Phelps still peremptorily forbade entrance: the whole rubbish must be removed, he said, before any further investigation could be entered upon.

Load after load; barrowful after barrowful: very nearly all gone now. A few minutes' more work and the business would be a *fait accompli*. And certainly, up to the present time, the result seemed to justify the surmise of the Hastings superintendent; who was of course present. Nothing whatever to repay this protracted search: nothing but the arch and passage; and they promised little enough. It might as well have been left alone! "Pretty much as I told you, sir," he observed in a low tone to one of the magistrates.

Nothing whatever. So it still seemed, when the shovels of the men, instead of burying themselves noiselessly in the loose mould, now struck with a dull thud on the earth-floor of the vault. So still, when even the few remaining barrow-loads were wheeled away, and the floor itself exposed to view, clean and bare. Still, apparently, nothing.

"Pretty much as I told you, sir," the superintendent again said, addressing the same magistrate as before, but this time in rather a higher key; but his remark did not elicit the nod and shrug of the shoulders it had previously done: it remained unheard. Mr. Phelps, who on the final clearance of the rubbish had stepped forward alone to the spot which it had lately occupied, desiring that every one else might remain in their places, was now stooping down, examining something.

The arch by which the passage discovered by Mr. Latrobe communicated with this portion of the caverns has been already often mentioned. It was of stone; and the stone, besides being let into the earth at the sides, was continued for some distance along the floor, forming a kind of pavement, the further end of which had been the last spot uncovered by the workmen. Mr. Phelps' movement forward had been almost simultaneous with the fall of the last spadeful of earth into the barrow;—a matter of one instant. But that instant had been sufficient.

"I thought so," he said, lifting himself up. "A pickaxe here. This stone has been disturbed not very long since."

The tool was brought, and Mr. Phelps himself

raised the stone, which gave way readily enough. He laid it, with great deliberation, against the wall on one side, and then took out something which had been concealed underneath it.

Difficult at first for the strained eyes of the bystanders to distinguish what this was. Something carefully and neatly folded : something still white in parts, but clotted, darkly and heavily, with blood, which the moisture of the soil had prevented from becoming wholly dry.

Mr. Phelps slowly unfolded this object, and then every one could see that it was a pocket-handkerchief. There was one corner to which the blood had not penetrated ; and in this corner it was also now palpable to all present that there was a name marked. Mr. Phelps, with the deliberation which had characterized all his movements, took out his spectacles, wiped them, and read the name.

" Charles Armitage." The name stitched in, in full.

The excitement caused by this discovery was arrested for a moment by the effect produced by it on Mr. Latrobe. The curate had borne much and manfully, but this confirmation of his worst fears acted too powerfully on the overcharged brain to be resisted; he had just strength to exclaim, "Unhappy boy," and then fell to the ground in a swoon.

One other person present did not remain to speculate on this fatal discovery. In the confusion caused by Mr. Latrobe's illness, the fisherman Ralph withdrew unobserved from the knot of spectators, and, quitting the caverns, made the best of his way through by-courts and alleys to his own home.

CHAPTER X.

THE preceding chapter will have put the reader in
possession of the facts which had occurred between
the time when Charles Armitage left Ralph's cottage,
and the unexpected appearance of the latter on the
beach under the East cliff, some two or three hours
later.   Ralph, as has been said, made his way to the
spot where Charles was lying, with precautions which
had attracted the notice of the latter even before he
discovered who his visitor actually was.

When he did so, his surprise was extreme.   He
started up from the shingle, and was about to speak ;
but the fisherman interrupted him.   Ralph's voice
and manner were stern, almost imperious.   " No,
Master," he said, " not that.   Maybe I've dooed what
I didn't ought to ; but I'll go through with it all the
same.   You can save yourself, if you like, young 'un
,

and you've just time for it. And just no more nor
time."

" Save himself ! "

Charles listened to the fisherman's words in an
utter bewilderment ; too great, at first, to allow of
his doing anything but echo them. " Save himself! "
What *could* Ralph mean ?

His visitor did not give him the opportunity of
putting the question in words, had he been capable of
doing so. " Yes, save yourself," Ralph continued ;
" that's plain enough, ain't it ? If it bean't, I'm not
a-going to make it plainer. Come, Master, you
needn't put on that dazed look, as if you knowed
nothing about the matter : they've been and found
it, that's all."

" Found it ! " Charles again echoed.

" Yes ; found that thing you hid under the stone
up yon :—Lord have mercy upon us ! Come, young
'un," he continued, seeing that Charles was about to
speak, " don't you go for to do that. You'd best
listen to what I've a got to say ; and don't say
nothink yourself : I should change my mind, if you
did, maybe, and that'd be worse luck for you. Now
look here : I've brought my boat round ; she's lying

just round the corner, in the little cove there; and
I'm a-going to take you off in her. You can get
across the beach as I did, keeping snug under the
bits of rock, and then nobody won't see you; and
on'st in her you lie down flat: and I've some tarpaulin
and things to cover you with. I'll **h**ang about till
dark, and nobody be none the wiser; and then you'll
be put aboard with the cap'en of a Yankeeman as I
knows, who'll ask no questions. We've saved a little
matter **of** gold, the old woman and I, and that'll stop
his mouth fast enough. He's off Dungeness now,
and starts to-morrow morning, sharp with the tide.
And then I've a done with you. Oh! Lord, Lord!"

What intuition, what lightning flash of intelligence was it which—long before Ralph had explained
his plan, almost before he had begun to speak in
answer to Charles's last exclamation of surprise—
darted through his hearer's brain; revealing to him,
in one instant, the position hitherto so unaccountably
concealed? Not the detail of it, of course. What had
been "found;" what had occurred since he last
parted from the fisherman, he could not comprehend: he did not attempt to. But he did comprehend
that something had happened;—and that as the

result of this, the charge which Helen had hitherto borne was now transferred to himself.

What intuition was this, have I said? That which outruns all other teachers, anticipates all other convictions, leaps to its goal instantly, unerringly ;—the intuition of love! " Thank Heaven, I can do something for her then," he murmured. The young, true heart had resolved, well-nigh before the brain had comprehended. Yes; he knew it all now :—the pointing, the whispering at street-corners, the shrugs of the shoulder, the undefined kind of "cutting," Mr. Latrobe's coldness; he knew what they all meant now.

And he also knew that he would bear them, ten times multiplied : bear even that darker result which might follow, to save *her*. Save her! ay, to shield her from the imputation even.

"I will not tell a lie," he thought, "even for that : I will not acknowledge myself guilty, by word or gesture. But I will stand still, and let them do what they like with me : that cannot be wrong. Most likely, even if I denied the thing, it would be no use ;—I don't know what has turned up, but Ralph seems to have made up his mind about it, and so I

suppose everybody else has. But at any rate, I will
not deny it : I should think not, indeed. All right,
Leonie dear."

He waited until Ralph had finished speaking, and
then replied in a low voice, but quite calmly,
" Thank you, Ralph. Thank you, old boy. But I will
stay here, Ralph; where I am."

The fisherman stood for some moments in absolute amazement. The perplexity of the scene might
have seemed ludicrous, but for the intense feeling
which wrought in the minds of both actors in it, and
elicited from its confusion the elements of a pathos
all the more tragic from its verging so closely on an
opposite sentiment. Charles could not wholly subdue
the outward indications of emotion ; his lip quivered,
and he shrunk from meeting the surprised look of his
humble friend, as actual guilt might have done.
Ralph, on his part, was moved by the coolness and
pluck of the criminal whom, with all his abhorrence
of the act itself, he was preparing to save from
justice ; but at the same time he was wholly at a loss
to account for the display of these qualities. He
spoke at last.

" It's your own affair, young 'un," he said,

doggedly. " It ain't *my* neck that'll run any risk by your being took. As far as that goes, I'd safest let the whole matter alone : ay, a long sight too. I haven't a ventured to tell the old 'ooman of what I meaned to do. I just took the bit of money out of our room; but she knowed nought about it : there'd have been a deal of words would have gone to that bargain, if she had. I daren't ask myself too many questions about it, for that matter. However, that's neither here nor there, young master," he continued. " Bide here—'where you are,' as you says,—if you must and will. If you do, you'll be took, and before many minutes too ; but that's your own business : I wash my hands of it."

Saying which, Ralph moved off towards his boat. He walked slowly, as if expecting to be called back every moment. The summons however did not come ; and as the fisherman neared the spot where the boat was moored, his discomposure at this reception of his offer vented itself in a gesture of irritation. " Cool as a nor'-wester," he muttered aloud. " One would think I'd come to tell him it was a day for us to go out with the lines, instead of offering to save his life. Says 'no' as off-hand as if he was one of your fine gents on the parade, who turn up their noses at you if there's a cat's-paw of wind on the water. 'Stay where I am,' indeed! You won't stop there long, my lad." And as Ralph spoke he began to untie the fastenings of the boat, deliberately enough as before. At the last moment however, Charles called after him.

"Ralph!"

"Well?" said the fisherman, sulkily. Charles made no answer, but moved towards the boat, where Ralph was still occupying himself with untying the knot, which he seemed to find specially difficult. Charles was now at the boat's-side.

"Well, sir?" said his companion once more.

"Ralph, old boy," said Charles, whose voice faltered in spite of himself; "we shall never meet again, most likely. I don't ask you to shake hands with me, for I do not see how you could do it. I only wanted . . wanted to know, if you ever do think of me hereafter, that you won't think more hardly than you can help. You're the only friend I have left, Ralph, and I mustn't call you that now: only, if you can, try not to think the worst of me."

"Well, sir, I'll try not," answered the fisherman.

" We've little enough call to do that of each other;
none of us haven't. And you've been a good friend
to both on us : one of ourselves like, as the Missus
always says. But oh ! sir, Mr. Armitage," Ralph
broke off, with an irrepressible look of dismay in his
weather-beaten face, " how *could* you go and do it :
how could you, Mr. Armitage ? A poor little child
like that ! And you that was so kind to every living
creature ! Oh ! Lord, Lord ! "

Charles made no answer, but walked slowly back
to the spot where Ralph had found him. He did not
pause now anywhere, but proceeded along the beach
in the direction of the town. The fisherman continued to look after him, until he had turned an
angle of the cliff and was lost to sight; he then
jumped into the boat, and hastily shoved off. There's
something about it all I can't understand," he
muttered; " not for the life of me. Yet it's plain
enough, too : in coorse he'd have denied it, if he
could. It ain't no use caring about it." And as a
commentary on his own words, Ralph threw himself
on one of the seats, and, letting the boat drift where
it would, sobbed like a child.

✻   ✻   ✻   ✻   ✻   ✻

Charles's soliloquy, and his subsequent interview with the fisherman had occupied some time, and it was late in the afternoon before he was arrested. In the excited state of public feeling, the police authorities had taken precautions to avoid attracting attention; and having ascertained that he had proceeded in the direction of the beach, despatched a couple of officers in plain clothes to the spot. Charles had returned as far as the outskirts of the town, and there remained, awaiting the arrival of the constables who he was aware would be sent in quest of him. He obeyed their summons at once, and, being handcuffed, was placed in a carriage which had been kept in waiting near at hand, and conveyed to the magistrates' room. Some of the latter had hastily met there, in anticipation of the arrest.

Thus far the arrangements had been effected quietly enough, few persons having been aware of what was going on; but when the carriage stopped, and Charles was taken indoors in custody of the police, the news spread like wild-fire. The room itself, and every avenue leading to it, were in a few minutes occupied by a breathless and eager crowd; while those who were excluded collected outside in

numbers which filled the narrow street from end to
end. An impulse was soon given to the mob thus
assembled; and the silence of expectation was
followed by loud and indignant cries, almost yells.
" Young coward! Wanted his sister to stand in his
shoes! Shame! Swing him up!" Such were
some of the exclamations which broke from the
crowd without; who were exasperated to the last
degree by Charles's conduct in exposing Helen to
suffer for the crime which it was believed was now
conclusively brought home to himself.

To the tumult which thus reigned out of doors,
the quietness of the proceedings in the magistrates'
room offered a marked contrast. They were in fact
simple and brief enough. The depositions were first
taken as to the circumstances connected with the
finding of the handkerchief marked with Charles's
name. They then went on to state the discovery of
the passage which led from the West Hill caverns to
the curate's lodgings; and which, on being explored,
as it soon was, offered a ready explanation of the
mode in which the perpetrator must have obtained
ingress to the former. Mrs. Graves and Mr. Latrobe,
who had been requested to be in attendance, as

being respectively the proprietor and occupant of the
lodgings, were then examined as to their knowledge
of such a passage existing, and the mode, if any,
in which Charles could have become acquainted with
the same fact.

Mrs. Graves' examination was soon terminated.
She had always understood that there was a disused
cellar adjoining the lodgings; but it had been
boarded up before her late husband and herself came
to the house, and she was wholly ignorant of there
having been any communication between it and the
spot where the body had been found.

The curate's deposition lasted longer, and was
listened to with breathless interest. Truthfully, and
without disguise, but with a wrung heart and choked
utterance, he detailed to the bench, in reply to the
questions addressed to him by the chairman, the
circumstances with which the reader is already
familiar. His manner elicited the warm sympathy
of all present. When the deposition was completed,
and Mr. Latrobe, with an anguish which he could
not disguise, bowed his head upon his arm and wept
audibly, the Chairman addressed to him a few words,
which expressed the unanimous feeling of the room.

" We are aware, sir," he said, " of your position as
this young man's late tutor, and entirely respect the
emotion you have shown. Had it been possible, we
should gladly have spared you the necessity of
coming forward; but the circumstances which have
thus singularly connected your apartments with this
act of violence made it imperative that you should
do so. You may have the consolation of knowing,
however, that the result would have been the same
even without your evidence. The discovery made
this afternoon would have compelled us to send the
case for trial in any event; and during the last few
minutes I have been given to understand that there
is also some further evidence forthcoming. A
deposition by one of the servants in the house, I
think you said?" the magistrate continued, addressing
the clerk who sat underneath him.

" Yes, sir."

" Is the person present ? "

A footman in Mrs. Armitage's employ here stepped
forward, and, with evident reluctance, stated that
some months since he had heard Mr. Charles speak
of the deceased child in a way which sounded like a
menace. He was in the pantry, cleaning the plate,

when Mr. Charles passed the window with Miss Helen ;—going on to the lawn, where there was an archery meeting. There was a belt of shrubs in front of the pantry window, but the words were quite audible :—"If that youngster doesn't come to an untimely end some day it won't be his own fault." Here Miss Helen had stopped him; but he added a minute after, in a curious kind of tone, muttering like, "Shouldn't wonder, for that matter, if I did it myself some day."

The deponent, at the Chairman's request, repeated the words ; which he did with only trifling variation : he was not clear as to one or two of them, he said ; but he was quite sure of their meaning. He thought at the time they implied a threat, and thought so still ; but he had not said anything about them before to-day : had almost forgotten them, in fact, until he heard about Mr. Charles this afternoon, and then he couldn't help speaking about them to the other servants. He hadn't wanted to come down here himself, but the others made him.

And so closed this new deposition ;—made in simple good faith, and, with one exception, entirely correct. A very trifling exception, as far as language

went; merely the substitution of one word of two
letters for another: "it" for "so;" but an all-
important one in its results:—converting into an
expression of deliberate malice towards another,
words which Charles, with the presentiment of the
afternoon when they were uttered strong upon him,
had used in reference to a foreseen destiny for
himself.

No one else came forward; and Charles, having
declined to make any statement in reply to the
charge, was formally committed for trial, and with
great difficulty removed from the room and into the
carriage. It was fortunate that the popular feeling
had vented itself in the cries with which the street
rung during his examination; had this not been the
case, the police could hardly have secured him from
violence. As it was, the crowd gradually made way
for the vehicle, following it only with some harmless
missiles, and with a storm of renewed execrations.

Once clear of the street, the carriage proceeded at
a rapid pace, and the same evening Charles was
lodged in the county gaol at Lewes; where the
commission for the spring assizes was to be opened
in the week following.

Not for one moment, during the examination in
the magistrates' room, the passage through the mob,
or the weary journey which followed it, had Charles
wavered in his resolution. Not even for the bitter-
ness of the thought, for the first time suggested to
him by the cries with which he had been assailed,
that he must bear, not only the penalty of the crime,
but the odium of having allowed Helen to be charged
with it in his place ! Involuntarily, and forgetting
for an instant that the imputation must rest on himself, Charles' cheek burned and his fist clenched at
the thought of such dastardly cowardice. Then he
half-smiled at his own excitement. " Yes, even
this," he murmured ; " even this, Leenie dear. You
shall know, perhaps, when all is over : I think *you*
will believe me, and there is no one else to care
about it. But at any rate, it shall be all right for you,
poor child."

And then, by an irresistible impulse, Charles'
thoughts turned from the consideration of his own
position, to a review of the facts which had been
deposed to before the magistrates, and which formed
such a singular chain of circumstantial evidence
against himself. The feeling which was thus aroused

soon predominated over every other. How had the
perpetrator, whoever it was, discovered that concealed
entrance to the scene of the crime which had so long
and successfully baffled detection? How had the
same person obtained possession of the trivial article
of dress which had afforded a presumption of his own
guilt as strong as it was in fact erroneous? Above
all, who was this perpetrator?

Alas! this latter query was the most painfully
absorbing of all. Turn it which way he would, the
same terrible thought perpetually recurred to his
mind. Difficult as it was to account for other
features in the case, and in the narrative which he
had that morning listened to (with a surprise far
exceeding that of any other person present) there
was one circumstance which forced itself on Charles'
mind with fatal prominence :—that long-hidden
witness; that handkerchief! How or when it had
been taken, he had no conception ; but could there,
alas, be any doubt as to who had taken it? Did not
every conclusion point the same way? Was it
not too evident that it must have been Helen?

And oh! how terrible was the reality thus forced
upon him! Resolute, more than ever resolute to

shield her; to avert from her—and if necessary, at
the cost of his own life—even the continued suspicion
of the act in which (as he believed) the aberration of
fever had involved, not her will or consent, but
unquestionably her hand! But how terrible it was
to reflect that this was the fact !   How startling was
this new confirmation of it !

One after another, Charles' thoughts travelled
over these topics in hopeless and monotonous dejection.   It was nearly morning before his mind,
wearied with ceaseless speculation, relaxed its
efforts, and consigned him to a feverish and broken
sleep.

CHAPTER XI.

IT was some hours after Charles' arrest before the intelligence reached Helen; who still, in the absence of any more suitable residence before surrendering on her bail, occupied the rooms placed at her disposal by Mrs. Armitage. The news was brought her by one of the maids at the Villa; who, on being questioned, detailed to her at length, and with tolerable fidelity, the varied occurrences of the morning, ending in Charles' examination and committal.

Helen's manner on hearing this underwent a marked change. She started from her seat with vehemence, and desiring the girl to wait, wrote a few hurried lines to Mr. Latrobe, begging him to come to the house without a moment's delay.

The note was despatched and found the curate in his lodgings. His main thought after quitting the

magistrates' room, had been how best to communicate the afternoon's occurrences to Helen; and
although the few lines she had sent made no reference
to these, he surmised that she had heard the news,
and was glad to be spared the necessity of being the
first to break it.

Hastily obeying the summons, Mr. Latrobe
followed the maid to the Villa, and found Helen in
the upstairs sitting-room in which he had previously
seen her. She was not seated, but pacing the room
up and down with an appearance of extreme agitation.

"Mr. Latrobe," she exclaimed, as he entered;
"oh! I am so glad you are come."

"'Mr. Latrobe,' Helen!" the curate echoed in
some dismay.

"Never mind that, dear," Helen answered; "I
did not mean it."

Mr. Latrobe clasped the beautiful but trembling
girl to his heart, imploring her to calm herself.
"You cannot bear it, dearest," he said; "you are
still far from strong."

"Do not mind me, Jean; only him. Save him
at once: at once, Jean. There must be some terrible
mistake somewhere."

"You have heard what has happened then?" the curate asked. "I was coming up to tell you, as soon as I could shape the words."

"Yes, yes, I have heard everything. And now do not lose a moment's time. I ought not perhaps to have sent for you in this way," Helen continued, slightly blushing; "but I have something very important to tell you. At least it may be important: I do not know; but at any rate, it is necessary that it should be now told. Mr. Latrobe, I saw him . . . Mr. Fortescue, in the house that night!"

The curate started to his feet in unfeigned astonishment. "Mr. Fortescue!" he repeated. In spite of his own love, and of the intelligence which, with all its trouble, beamed in the bright steady eye which encountered his own, he could not help for an instant recalling the apprehensions expressed by Mr. Sims. Was this delusion? Was it the indication of a mind permanently affected by the delusion, and still reproducing the wandering imageries and fatal tenacity of an insane conviction?

The anguish of this thought was intolerable, and Mr. Latrobe writhed under it. Apparently Helen

divined its cause. "You must think I am still
light-headed," she said ; "but I will be quite calm
now, and then you shall judge for yourself : only
let us lose no time, Jean. I have long felt that there
is some extraordinary mystery about this matter ;
but as long as I was the only sufferer, I had not the
fortitude to disclose what I have now done. I had
small encouragement, in fact, to do so, even if there
had been no other reason. I did, on my first
recovery, mention it to Mr. Sims, on his solemn
assurance of secrecy ; but I saw that he utterly
disbelieved me : he thought I was still raving in
fever. His reception of what I said had such an
effect upon me that tortures would not have forced
the secret from me again. It would not have been
mere incredulity, too, it would have met with : you
know what people would have said about . . . about
my going on thinking of him, as they would have
called it. I would have died rather than have undergone that. But they may say what they like now.
Sit down, Jean, and I will tell you all about it."

Mr. Latrobe obeyed, stealing an arm in support
of the fair slight form, which still shook with its
emotion. Helen proceeded.

" You recollect, of course, all about that evening?"

" The night of the . . . that is of the poor boy's disappearance ? "

" Yes. As I told the magistrates, I was downstairs at that time, in poor Fred's room. I told them why I went there; that I did not find him there, as I expected; that I left the room by the door at the foot of the stairs, meaning to return to my own."

" And you did not return : not, that is, for an hour and upwards; of course, I recollect all this perfectly. But, good heavens, Helen! Do you mean, . . mean that . . . . Impossible ! "

" Listen, Jean. I mean that as I placed my foot on the first step I saw Mr. Fortescue in the hall, at no great distance. He did not see, or rather did not recognize me :—see me he did, for he was looking full towards the staircase, and drew back immediately; but I do not think he distinguished who I was. I had moved quickly, and probably the staircase would have prevented his seeing more than my dress. But *his* face I saw most plainly : and Mr. Fortescue it was ; beyond all doubt or question."

" But, Helen, consider : he had just married ; and I know they were in Yorkshire at that time,

at his family seat: they had returned there after
spending the honeymoon abroad. Helen, dearest,
this is of immense importance: are you quite sure?"

"Quite sure, Jean: as sure as that you are now
scated by me. All the more sure, because he was
most singularly dressed; in sailor's clothes. Not
the sort of jacket which gentlemen often wear down
here in the summer, but a rough dress, just like one
of the fishermen: something in which I had never
seen him. But for this, I might have fancied it was
some trick of the eye, or the fancy; especially when
my illness came so soon afterwards. But it was no
trick, no mistake, Mr. Latrobe; it was as certain as
that I now speak and you hear: as certain as that
the sun rises and the tides ebb and flow. It was its
being so certain that brought on that attack of
fever: it preyed upon my mind from that moment.

"As I told the magistrates," Helen continued,
"I was utterly terrified; much too terrified to go
on upstairs. I turned back at once, and hid behind the baize door leading to the bath-room. I
hardly knew what I was doing, or how long I stopped
there : I had no notion of the time until, as I told
them, I heard the curfew ; and that I had forgotten

until the Chairman pressed me. Jean," Helen again
continued after a pause, almost shrinking even from
the loving arm which encircled her, " it was not
merely the seeing him ; or the seeing him there, at
that time and in such a disguise, which frightened
me so. It was something in his face, of which, as
I have said, I had a complete view : something which
I have never seen in any other human face. You
recollect what a powerfully deep and expressive eye
he always had. But when I then met him, it was
preternatural : it was just as if a corpse had sat up
and looked at me. It haunted me for days and weeks
afterwards ; it does now, at times. When I fled up
to my room, as I told the Chairman ;—venturing out
on the staircase at last,—that eye seemed to follow
me : to fasten upon me wherever I turned. Charles
was there, as I remember, but I hardly noticed him ;
could not answer when he spoke ; could not have
told when he left the room. All through my sleep
that night, all the next day, that look fascinated me.
It was quite true what Burgess said. I did afterwards
feel drawn irresistibly to the spot where I had thus
met Mr. Fortescue ; could not force myself away from
it ; came back to it again and again.

" And then, when the fever came on, there was
the same thing all through it, night and day—that
intolerable look ! It seemed of the very substance of
the delirium itself; torturing me; peering through
and through my thoughts. I kept fancying that I
was in a house with an immense number of rooms,
and was trying to hide myself in one of them ; but
as soon as I entered it, there was his eye upon me
again, driving me on hopelessly and incessantly. I
told Mr. Sims because I wanted to know if I had said
anything about it in my delirium ; but the effort of
doing so was horrible. But I will tell everything
now ; as and when it may be thought necessary. Only
be quick, Jean."

Mr. Latrobe pondered for a minute or two, and
then said, hesitatingly, " Of course I believe what
you say, Helen dear : believe it fully and entirely.
But still I can't comprehend it ; even allowing him to
have been there. Do you mean ; do you mean,"
Mr. Latrobe repeated, lowering his voice, " that he,
Mr. Fortescue, had anything to do with that . . that
he was the person who did it ? "

" Don't ask me, Jean," Helen replied, with great
agitation. " I know nothing, can guess nothing ;

cannot bear to think of it even : it is all some horrible
mystery. It is only just now, since I heard about
Charles, that such an idea has crossed my mind. I
never thought of connecting the two things before :
I cannot now : it is too dreadful. Dreadful enough
for me, after what is past, to have to state the fact
at all ; feeling that others will draw from it the same
inference in regard to him—to Mr. Fortescue—which
you have done. But there is no help for it : that
must be told, and everything : everything in the
world that can throw light upon what occurred on
that unhappy night. Mr. Latrobe," continued Helen,
turning suddenly to her companion, "you do not
doubt that Charles is wholly and absolutely innocent,
do you ? I know," she added, "that you could not
help saying what you did to-day before the magistrates : it was your duty to do it, even if it had
not been forced from you. But you do not yourself
doubt him : your own heart and judgment do
not ? "

Mr. Latrobe paused some little time before he
replied. " No, Helen," he then said ; " I do not, if
you do not. Woman's instinct is often clearer in
such matters than ours. That I did doubt and

suspect him most grievously, even before to-day, I freely confess to you. Ever since my return from Ireland the suspicion has been a terrible burden to me; and, viewed as a matter of reason, it would be greatly augmented by the discovery of this afternoon. But if you have no fears in regard to him, I will have none."

"Oh! then, Jean," Helen exclaimed, clasping her hands almost in supplication, "have none. Have none, whatever may happen; not even if the apparent presumptions against him were multiplied twenty times. If such a thought should ever cross your mind, drive it away like a sin. There is not a being on the face of the globe, not an angel in Paradise, more clear from this guilt than Charles is. Dear, dear Charles! Jean," continued Helen, passionately, "I do love you! I do indeed, for your own sake. But I will love you as never woman did, if you can rescue him. I cannot account, any more than you can, for that thing which has been found to-day, or for several other things: they are part of the mystery in which the whole matter is wrapped; only I do know that Charles is wholly innocent. And now go, Jean," Helen added; "let Mr. Rigwell at once know what I have told you. Whatever it means, whatever the consequences may be, it must not be a secret one hour longer."

A few minutes afterwards, Mr. Latrobe quitted the Villa, and proceeded to the lawyer's house. The vehemence with which Helen had urged Charles' cause had, for the present at any rate, fairly overmastered the curate's previous convictions. Even had this been otherwise, he had promised to share her undoubting belief in her brother's innocence, and he was determined to be loyal to his word. He therefore made the best of his way to the house, impelled at the same time by no ordinary feeling of curiosity to know how the disclosure which Helen had just made to him would be entertained by a third mind.

The evening had fallen for some time, and Mr. Rigwell, having despatched his work for the day, was just sitting down to a quiet rubber in his own drawing-room. He obeyed the curate's summons however, and desiring lights to be brought to the office, awaited the important communication which Mr. Latrobe promised he was about to make.

" Something connected with to-day's occurrences,

I conclude," said the lawyer. "The plot seems thickening around us every hour."

"There is a very strange element imported into it now," said Mr. Latrobe, "whatever results may follow from it: a wholly new actor brought upon the stage. Miss Armitage just now sent for me, of her own accord, and gave me a full statement of what occurred during the period of her absence from her own room on the night of the child's abstraction."

"Ay, ay, really? I hope you are at liberty to divulge it."

"I came here for the express purpose, and at her own request. You know already, as I collected from Mr. Sims soon after my return home, and as the public also know through Miss Armitage's own statement, that she saw something which terrified her so much as to detain her out of her room all that time; but of which she refused to give any explanation. Now she has told me what this was. On her way upstairs she saw Mr. Fortescue."

"Whe—ew," whistled the lawyer, throwing himself back in his chair, and thrusting his hands into his pockets. "Saw Mr. Fortescue!" he added, after recovering from the extremity of his first surprise.

"You might as well say she saw Oliver Cromwell. How could she? He was up at his place in the north, just married. I saw it all in the *Times*."

"It is the fact, Mr. Rigwell, notwithstanding," said the curate.

"The fact! How can it be the fact? It's utterly impossible. What evidence is there of it?"

"The young lady's own statement," said Mr. Latrobe with some little asperity.

"Well, well, we will not quarrel about it," said the lawyer; who, although not fully apprised of the present relations between his visitor and Helen, was aware of their general tendency. "I am perfectly satisfied, Mr. Latrobe, that our fair client believes she saw whatever she says she did, whether it be possible or not. Let me hear the entire detail, as far as you have been put in possession of it."

Thus solicited, Mr. Latrobe recapitulated to the attorney the communication which Helen had recently made to him. Mr. Rigwell listened thoughtfully, and with extreme interest. When his visitor had ceased, he did not at once reply but sat nursing his knee in silence for some minutes.

"On the whole," he said at last, "I think it

easier to accept this as fact than to account for it on any other theory. You must pardon my first reception of your announcement; which you must admit was sufficiently startling. Looking at the case medically I should be of Sims's opinion. I should surmise that there was some trace of the young lady's indisposition still subsisting : some delusion, natural enough under the circumstances, and likely to be more or less permanent as her general health and spirits might improve, or the reverse. Looking at it popularly, again ;—from the point of view at which the intelligence of an ordinary hearer, or the extraordinary intelligence peculiar to a jury of twelve enlightened Englishmen would view it—I should say that there was neither delusion nor mystery about the matter; but merely the every-day quality which disposes a love-lorn damsel—you must pardon my bluntness, my dear sir,—who has been slighted by the object of her affections, to conjure up his image at times and places when it is neither opportune nor physically possible. But looking at the matter as a lawyer and a practical man, I feel bound to say that it deserves our most serious attention; especially in the present position. In Miss Armitage's own case

you see, notwithstanding the committal, which I take
to have been wrong, a conviction was impossible : I
do not think that the grand jury can even find a bill.
But, bless my soul, it is another matter now, with
this young man. It is life and death to him. We
must leave no stone unturned."

" And you think this circumstance then deserving
further inquiry?" asked the curate.

" Most unquestionably, my dear sir. What particularly strikes me about it is the young lady's
reticence : her persistent reticence on the matter up
to the present moment; when, for the first time, she
makes the disclosure for a specific purpose. This
seems to me a feature wholly inconsistent with either
delusion or the effects of a disordered imagination.
People never deal rationally with an irrational belief.
They may talk, or dream, or otherwise cheat themselves
into the acceptance of something as fact which is not
fact; but they are wholly incapable of acting in regard
to it as they would in regard to facts which are really
such : the taint of the original mispersuasion clings
to the matter throughout. But in this case nothing
can be more sensible than the young lady's proceedings. She mentioned the circumstance at the earliest

moment of her recovery to her medical adviser. She did so with a special object, which she accordingly attained; and finding, from his reception of her story, that it would be discredited if repeated elsewhere, she forbore to do so, promising you at the same time that it should be disclosed if necessary. Now, at this present conjuncture, circumstances have arisen which make the disclosure imperative, or highly desirable; and of her own accord she sends for you and places it in your hands to deal with as you think best. I see in all this strong indications of fact :—it means business. That the alleged circumstance is in itself wholly astounding and unintelligible, referable to no known or even possible motive; that it adds another link to the already numerous complications of the business, is true enough. But this is no reason for our not making the most of it."

"You think then," asked the curate, "that we should at once communicate Miss Armitage's statement to the proper authorities, whoever they may be?"

"On no account, my dear sir. It would be wholly useless to do so at present; would entirely destroy any point in the young man's favour which may be made out of it at the trial. It would simply be disbelieved ;—as I have said, attributed to the fancy or incipient delirium of a love-sick girl. No; let us at once endeavour to obtain corroborative evidence of the fact. It may not avail us, even if we do; may not materially further the young man's case. Even if Mr. Fortescue was in the house as stated, it does not follow that he was the guilty party. His visit might be referable to some remorseful feeling in regard to the young lady whom he had wronged; some overpowering desire to see her again at all hazards : certainly not more improbable than his having been in any way concerned in this object-less crime. Still, allowing full weight to all this, it is impossible to deny that his presence there at all, at that precise hour and in such a disguise, if it can be established *aliunde,* is a most important circum-stance : most suspicious and extraordinary, beyond a doubt."

" How do you propose then to procure the further evidence you speak of ? " asked the curate.

" By setting as many ferrets as I can on the track, Mr. Latrobe. You leave that to me. If the man came all the way from Yorkshire down here he must have left some traces of his journey; must have

been seen by somebody, somewhere. It is not so
many weeks since, after all : the scent will be warm
still. You leave me to manage that. Happily there
are plenty of funds ; for as you know, the result of
the child's death under twenty-one was that that
iniquitous will fell to the ground, and the old man's
property descended to Charles as his rightful heir.
All the worse for the poor boy's case in one way ; but
it will help us in following up this clue, which will be
costly work enough. Not but that I would have
undertaken it out of my own pocket, had it been
otherwise," added the lawyer ; whose kindness of
heart no less than his professional interest was
beginning to be powerfully enlisted in the matter.

" But will not this take some time ? " asked Mr.
Latrobe.

" Time ! yes indeed. I must get about it at once.
I will arrange my plan of proceeding this very night."

" The assizes are very close," continued the
curate, still hesitating ; " would it not be better at
least to have Miss Armitage's deposition taken at
once, and then prosecute our inquiries ? Even if
you succeed in obtaining the evidence you wish, it
might be too late : the trial might be over."

" It would not make a bit of difference," replied
Mr. Rigwell. " A reprieve would be granted immediately upon an affidavit of the facts, and the matter
could be investigated quite as well then as previously.
But there is no fear of my being late : if anything
turns up, I shall be ready with it in ample time.
Don't let's prejudice our case, Mr. Latrobe, by giving
the public even a hint of it at present. After the
first surprise they would go talking it over, and by
the time the assizes came would so fully have
persuaded themselves that it was all moonshine, that
no corroborative circumstances would be of any use.
No, no; let me get the case cleanly and properly
patched up : facts dovetailed in ; presumptions made
the most of ; then we'll come upon them with it as a
grand *coup* at the trial itself. Take my word for it,
my dear sir, I am right."

Mr. Latrobe was not wholly convinced, but felt
bound to defer to professional knowledge, and left the
ttorney to arrange his proceedings accordingly.

CHAPTER XII.

THERE was one person who was still less satisfied than the curate when the interview with Mr. Rigwell was reported to her next morning; and that was Helen Armitage. Surely, she remonstrated, this delay cannot be necessary. Let my statement be taken for what it is worth only, but let it be made public at once. Why should Charles lie for an hour under an imputation even; from which, as Mr. Rigwell himself allows, he may possibly be cleared by this disclosure?

Gradually, but still very reluctantly, Helen allowed herself to be reasoned into the attorney's view, that, for Charles' own sake, the revelation of this new and most important feature in the case should be deferred until it could be made with decisive effect. Finally she consented; but on one condition, only. "Up to the conclusion of the trial," she said, "I will keep this matter to myself, as you desire I shall. Let the evidence against Charles be gone through; the case, as they will endeavour to make it out, be concluded. If by that time Mr. Rigwell is in a position to produce the counter-evidence, as he calls it; if he has collected the necessary materials for that purpose, by all means let him do so : I will place myself in his hands unreservedly. But if he is not then ready, I will step forward to be spokeswoman myself. Charles' safety, as well as his name and honour, are too important to be risked, even to the extent of a mistaken verdict, as long as I can do anything to prevent it. Although a prisoner myself, I will insist on being heard : on the whole truth being told, intensely painful as it will be to me personally. You promise me, Jean Latrobe, that you and Mr. Rigwell will arrange this for me ? "

The curate gave the required assurance; and, after some discussion, it was further arranged between him and Helen that Charles should not be informed of the disclosure made by the latter, or the researches which Mr. Rigwell was preparing to institute in consequence, as it might only inspire hopes which might not be realized.

Things accordingly went on, during the nine or ten days which still elapsed before the commencement of the Lewes assize, with little alteration as regarded either of the persons principally interested in its result. Helen remained at Harcourt Villa, constantly visited by Mr. Latrobe, and receiving from him the support which her uncontrollable anxiety upon Charles' account made requisite. Charles himself was closely confined at Lewes. The only special circumstance noticeable in regard to him was that he positively refused to communicate, either personally or by letter, with any one who could be supposed to feel solicitude as to the result of his trial, or the line of defence he was prepared to adopt upon it. To arrange for the latter, Mr. Rigwell, before departing upon his own investigations, had despatched his managing clerk to Lewes, with instructions to offer Charles every assistance in his power, and obtain such materials as he could for the guidance of the counsel whom Mr. Rigwell was desirous of retaining in his behalf. This gentleman Charles peremptorily declined to see. Mr. Latrobe had no better success, when, at Helen's solicitation, as well as under the influence of strong and contending feelings in his own mind, he endeavoured on one or two occasions· during this period to obtain an interview with his late pupil. Each time Charles sent a verbal message, thanking him kindly, but requesting that he would not press to see him.

The only person whom Charles did see,—and this more in accordance with the prison regulations than with his own wish,—was the chaplain, who paid him several visits. Charles received these respectfully, but declined to avail himself for the present of the clergyman's ministrations; still more, to touch in any way on the subjects connected with his own arrest and imprisonment. From each of these interviews the chaplain retired with increased perplexity. Nothing was less like obduracy or hardihood than Charles' demeanour, and yet nothing less like contrition. At times, there was a look almost of satisfaction about him, which wholly baffled the visitor's analysis; especially when succeeded, as it would be in the next moment, by one of intense sadness. It was an equally-balanced impossibility from such data to infer either guilt or innocence.

To the comparative quiet into which the parties mainly interested had thus temporarily subsided, Mr. Rigwell's activity meanwhile offered a marked contrast. His researches were prosecuted with the utmost energy, sparing neither time, labour, nor outlay. Three hours' work in London had the effect of starting upon the necessary inquiry an equal number of detectives, as they would now be termed, who pursued their investigations independently of each other, although on such a plan as to converge to a general result.

Swiftly but stealthily, with the keenness and vigilance of their craft, the experts followed up the scent.

It was quickly ascertained that Mr. Fortescue had in fact been absent from Dalemain at the time when the crime was committed, and for a period before and after it amply sufficient to have allowed of his visiting Hastings in the meantime.

Inspirited by this result as far as it went, Mr. Rigwell and those acting under his instructions proceeded with new alacrity. As a matter of course their first inquiries were made at Hastings itself. These however proved utterly fruitless. The persons to whom they were addressed had seen no one answering Mr. Fortescue's description, either in his own dress or in the disguise which Helen stated him to have assumed, at any time coinciding with that of Fred's removal from the Villa. This entailed upon the inquirers the necessity of proving from the other end, if possible, that Mr. Fortescue had in fact paid —if he ever had—this mysterious visit to the town.

From Dalemain, the detectives charged with this portion of the search easily followed Mr. Fortescue to the Wastdale farm-house; his journey to Cumberland having been prosecuted, as the reader will recollect, without any motive for concealment. At the farm, they learned the particulars of his visit there. He was a favourite with the inmates, and the details of this were readily communicated, as well as many other matters bearing on Mr. Fortescue's general habits and character ; but nothing which could suggest a motive either for his journey to Hastings, or for his being concerned in a crime of such atrocity. The occupants of the farm thought him eccentric, but not more so than they were prepared to expect in any one who had unlimited wealth and leisure at his command, and had been for many years " in foreign parts." They mentioned his having walked to Deep Ghyll on the last day of this recent visit, but of course no clue could be extracted from this; although the farmer's wife had noticed his manner on his return from the spot as being unusually excited, and had seen a light in his room, and heard him moving there several times during the night following. It had in fact struck her, although she could not say positively that it was so, that the bed had not been slept in that night :—apparently it had, but she was not satisfied that the clothes had not been purposely so arranged. Beyond this, nothing was extracted of the slightest importance.

This divergence to Cumberland having been wholly unexpected by Mr. Rigwell in laying out his original plans, some reconstruction of the latter became necessary, and two valuable days were lost in consequence. The new arrangements however having been then effected, the attorney and those acting with him proceeded with redoubled activity, to make up for the time thus sacrificed.

It will be recollected that on leaving Wastdale Mr. Fortescue had not gone direct to London, but had purposely travelled by cross roads; occasionally walking part of the distance, so as to throw as much difficulty as possible in the way of any one endeavouring to ascertain what route he had in fact taken. So skilfully had this been done as greatly to baffle the persons now following up his track; not ultimately precluding their discovery of it, but retarding the inquiry, and often compelling them to retrace their own steps and begin afresh after being misled by a false clue. A further difficulty arose from their uncertainty as to the period at which Mr. Fortescue had assumed the rough boatman's dress in which Helen stated she had seen him. As this might have been done in any portion of the journey, it was necessary to inquire for him under this disguise as well as in his ordinary costume; and erroneous intelligence was often unintentionally given and acted upon in consequence.

Eventually, the pursuit proved successful as far as London; but this result had only been obtained at a most serious outlay of the limited time at Mr. Rigwell's disposal; while, on reaching the metropolis, it seemed as if the labour and perplexity of the search had only just to commence. The precautions which had been taken here by Mr. Fortescue proved most

baffling. No trace of his movements was to be
obtained at the offices of the Hastings coaches, or of
any others running in the same direction. Any
information as to his having been seen elsewhere in
London was obviously hopeless: the few inquiries
which were made with this object only served to show
their utter futility. Nor could the faintest tidings
of him be obtained along any of the roads by which
he could be supposed to have proceeded to Hastings.
This was mainly owing to the further disguise which
Mr. Fortescue had worn in this portion of his journey;
and in which it will be remembered Helen had *not*
seen him:—the false whiskers, which he had purchased
in town and had purposely removed when he assumed
the fisherman's dress he ultimately wore. The
transformation thus made in his appearance was
total; and few indeed, even of those who had known
him personally, could have recognized him with this
alteration. To add to the complications already
existing, a subsequent inquiry at one of the coach-
offices in St. Martin's-le-grand—undertaken almost
in desperation, and with only the vague hope of something favourable turning up—led to the accidental
discovery of Mr. Fortescue having taken his place by

the Hertford mail; which he had done in his own name. This indeed failed of its immediate object; as the evident marks of a design to elude pursuit in the mode of his journey as far as London made it probable that this was intended as a mere blind : as it in fact was, to meet the possibility of a search being commenced in London in the first instance. Still it involved further delay. It was impossible not to exhaust the contingencies arising from this circumstance, however little might be their real value. This was accordingly done, the result being that Mr. Fortescue was found to have alighted at Hertford that evening; although as to his subsequent return to London, or any trace of his journey between the latter place and Hastings, the pursuers remained as much at fault as ever.

At length, after the lapse of some further priceless days, the trail was struck. At various points of Mr. Fortescue's possible route in Kent and Sussex, sometimes in one county and sometimes in the other, and, in each, along roads apparently wholly disconnected, a person had been met, answering his general description in height, figure, ordinary dress, and other particulars; although all the informants concurred in stating him to have worn whiskers. In most instances too he was seen apparently proceeding in a direction the reverse of that which would have taken him to Hastings. Gradually however the detectives became satisfied that this was Mr. Fortescue. The whiskers were an obvious form of disguise, and offered little difficulty to the police themselves, when the identification was complete in other respects; although they had prevented the persons to whom their inquiries were addressed from recognizing the object of them in the first instance. Nor did they attach much weight to the contradictory lines of route followed by Mr. Fortescue, as the uniformity of proceeding and evident purpose of concealment shown by this circumstance more than counterbalanced the presumption arising from it. Once satisfied in other respects that the person who thus acted was in fact the one they were in quest of, it was easy to divine that he had purposely allowed himself to be seen during the day, and had on each occasion made up the lee-way thus lost, as well as advanced a stage or two forward on his journey after nightfall.

The above result being once obtained, the piecing together of the main portions of Mr. Fortescue's journey between London and Hastings was a matter of comparatively little difficulty. What had to be done for this purpose was done skilfully and successfully.

* * * * *

It was early, still almost dark, on the morning of the day preceding that on which the assizes were to commence at Lewes, when Mr. Latrobe, who was still at Hastings, but intended to proceed to Lewes that afternoon, was roused by an impatient knocking at the private door leading up to his lodgings. Opening his window to ascertain the cause, the curate found Mr. Rigwell standing below, and at once admitted him. It was the first time he had seen the attorney since they parted on the evening of Helen's disclosure. To his numerous applications at the office the reply had still been the same : " Mr. Rigwell had not come home yet ; had not stated when he would : it was wholly uncertain." Nor had Mr. Latrobe been able to extract from the clerk, who probably was himself left in ignorance, any information as to the progress of the important mission with which Mr. Rigwell had charged himself. It was therefore with satisfaction proportioned to the anxiety with which he had been awaiting the arrival of news, that he now saw the latter enter his room.

"Congratulate me," said the lawyer, briskly : "congratulate me, my dear sir. Our work is almost done now."

"You have discovered something then ?" asked Mr. Latrobe.

"'Something!' my good friend; everything: almost everything, that is. Just about a couple of days more wanted: that is all, I believe; and that is just what we have got. I shall keep my promise to you, Mr. Latrobe: we shall have everything quite ready by the time the trial begins. Let me see, the assizes open to-morrow. The judges can't be in Lewes before the afternoon. Then they have to go to church; then afterwards all the preliminaries, the grand jury charged, and so on. No business can be transacted that evening, clearly; and the next forenoon will be occupied in finding the bill—if they do find it, as I suppose they will. The court will take some of the light cases meanwhile : there are plenty of them. The afternoon of the day after to-morrow is the very earliest at which our case can be called."

"But tell me, I entreat you," said Mr. Latrobe,

who had been impatiently listening to the lawyer's detail, "what has been discovered? Have you found any evidence of Mr. Fortescue having been at Hastings on that day?"

"Well, that is precisely the one thing left to do," said Mr. Rigwell; "or nearly so: the rest is substantially quite done. We have followed up the scent *secundum artem*, Mr. Latrobe; tracked him from earth to earth; from Yorkshire to Cumberland, Cumberland to London; London to Hastings, or just short of it. Such windings and turnings; such disguises; but all ineffectual. Every link in the chain is now complete; excepting two or three in the last section, between this and London, which I make no doubt of securing in the course of the next forty-eight hours: and excepting, as I have said, some corroborative evidence of his having been actually here, in Hastings itself. Having got everything else complete, I am most anxious to procure this: it will be the crowning touch and keystone of the whole. It has proved very difficult; but our entire success elsewhere will make us redouble our exertions in this quarter, and I make no doubt of being ultimately successful. And now, good morning, my dear sir.

My journey to-day must lie in two or three opposite directions, and I have no time to spare. Only got back here late last night, and snatched a few hours' sleep. Busy life we men of business lead, Mr. Latrobe." Saying which the attorney hurried down-stairs, and started on his further explorations.

CHAPTER XIII.

THE proceedings on a criminal trial are so familiar, and have been so often and graphically described for the information of those who are not acquainted with them, that it is unnecessary to detain the reader with any detailed account here.

As Mr. Rigwell had anticipated, no business of importance was transacted on the day which followed his last interview with Mr. Latrobe. The sittings in the Nisi Prius court were commenced, but none of the Crown cases were taken ; the judge who was to sit in the Criminal Court having been detained in the last assize town later than his colleague.

With regard to the day following, however, Mr. Rigwell's anticipations proved less correct. With the exception of the Hastings case, the criminal business at this assize was of an unusually light character. There were several prisoners for trial, and in this respect the attorney had been correctly informed; but the offences were mostly of a trivial character, and the business was rapidly despatched accordingly. Two or three of those charged, pleaded guilty and were sentenced to short further terms of imprisonment; in other cases, where evidence was taken, it was of a simple and direct character, and little time was occupied either in cross-examination or in finding a verdict. By twelve o'clock the whole criminal list was gone through, with the exception of the Hastings case and two or three others, in which an adjournment to a later hour had been requested; the counsel retained in them being engaged in the civil court.

Before the grand jury, meanwhile, the proceedings had been equally brief as regarded Charles; against whom a true bill was at once found, on hearing the evidence adduced by the prosecution. In Helen's case, on the other hand, the indictment was the subject of a protracted discussion. Ultimately it was arranged that, as her brother's trial would now come off immediately, the grand jury should adjourn to a later hour in the day; and the prosecution should then be at liberty to bring forward against her any facts adduced on the trial, or otherwise elicited in the course of it, which might raise an additional presumption against herself. By the time this was settled, the proceedings in court against Charles had commenced.

From a very early hour that morning the building had been densely crowded, in anticipation of this event. It was not large, and every possible and impossible place in it was occupied: from the galleries, the bar-seats, the reporters' bench, gang-ways and passages, nooks and corners of every description, scores of curious eyes awaited the arrival of the prisoner.

When he at last entered in the custody of two of the police, there was a profound stillness—awe-stricken almost—throughout the whole body of spectators. Every one present seemed occupied in recalling the magnitude of the crime, and, as it were, gauging the proportion which the person charged bore to it. The police then withdrew, and Charles was left alone in the dock, immediately in front of the judge; the bar-seats and some accommodation for the attorneys employed being

between them. The jury occupied a box on one
side, at right angles with the dock and the judges'
bench.   Immediately under Charles sat Mr. Latrobe
and Mr. Rigwell's clerk ; both of whom from time
to time cast anxious looks towards the curtain which
screened the public entrance, in the hopes that some
fortunate accident might bring the attorney himself
to Lewes earlier than the hour which his mis-
apprehension as to the probable time of the trial
coming on seemed to promise.

Soon after entering the court, while some
necessary formalities were being adjusted, Charles
leant forward and addressed some words to Mr.
Rigwell's clerk in a low voice ;—inaudible to any
but those seated near him, although every ear in
the building was strained to catch their import.
As already mentioned, Charles had hitherto declined
to hold any communication with the clerk, or to
permit him to take any steps for his defence; but
this gentleman, who was himself a practising attorney,
had attended in court in the event of his services
being accepted at the last moment.

Charles' communication however had no reference
to himself ;—it related solely to Helen.

"Had the grand jury found a true bill against her?" Charles asked.

The clerk explained to him the decision which had been come to in regard to the charge against Helen, and which he had heard just before entering the Court. Charles made no reply, but again stood up in the dock, waiting the commencement of the proceedings. His manner, although firm, was depressed; and the sympathy which had been at first elicited by his extreme youth, and by the dreadful situation in which he was now placed, began rapidly to ebb, as the spectators recalled the heinousness of the crime which had led to it.

This was still further the case, when, after a pause of some minutes, the clerk of arraigns called the prisoner by name to the bar of the court, "to answer the matter charged upon him in the indictment." Charles moved slightly forward to the front of the dock, and was then desired to hold up his hand, which he did.

The clerk of arraigns then, slowly and in a clear voice audible to all present, read the particulars of the indictment, charging him with the wilful murder of Frederick Poynder at Hastings in the County of Sussex,

on some day unknown, but then past, and specifying
the cause of death as found by the coroner's inquest.
Charles was then asked, "whether he was guilty of
the crime whereof he stood charged, or not guilty?"

The crowded auditory who sat, or stood, awaiting
his reply with the eager interest which attaches even
to the minutest particulars of such proceedings, and
even where no doubt is entertained of the prisoner
pleading the customary "Not Guilty," were on this
occasion disappointed. The question, or "demand"
as it is technically termed, remained unanswered.
The clerk of arraigns repeated it in a distinct and
somewhat peremptory tone, but still with the same
result. The judge then interposed.

"Do you hear the question that is put to you?"
he asked, addressing Charles.

"I do, my Lord," Charles answered, looking up
for the first time, and speaking in a clear but somewhat tremulous voice.

"And I conclude you understand it?"

"I do, my Lord," Charles again answered,

"Why then do you not plead to it? You are
required to state whether you are 'Guilty' or 'Not
Guilty,' which of the two are you?"

" I do not wish to plead either way," said Charles.

" That cannot be permitted," the judge answered.
" It is imperative that you should adopt one course
or the other."

" My Lord," said Charles, " I fear you will think
me obstinate and disrespectful ; and I hardly know
what to do to prevent my seeming so : but I must
abide by what I have said. I decline to plead
altogether."

The judge paused, and fixed a long and scrutiniz-
ing look on the prisoner before him.

" You say you understand the indictment you
have heard read," he asked at last.

" I do, my Lord," was Charles' answer again.

" You understand that it charges you with
wilful murder : the murder of a young helpless
child ? "

An involuntary shudder passed over the prisoner's
frame as the judge spoke. To the bystanders, by
most of whom it was plainly seen, it appeared to
furnish an additional presumption of guilt. They
might have changed their belief, had they known
the feeling to which that emotion was really due :
the thought which for the moment occupied Charles'

mind, to the exclusion of all concern as to his own position. "Poor little Leenie; poor child," he said to himself. "Heaven grant *she* may never hear that said : never hear those cruel words used of her own most involuntary act! She shall not, if I can help it." The next instant however Charles recovered himself, and replied to the question, almost without a pause—so rapid had been the reflection which has filled some lines in writing ;—"Yes, my Lord, I do understand that."

"Do you mean then," the judge continued, "that you cannot say whether you are guilty or not guilty of that dreadful crime ?"

"I did not say cannot," Charles answered.

"You mean that you will not then," asked the judge.

"Yes."

"Perhaps," the judge resumed after a pause, "you are not acquainted with the law in regard to this. Fortunately indeed for you, in one sense, the law has recently been altered. According to the old practice, the contumacy you now show would have subjected you to a barbarous treatment : a species of torture ; which would have been persisted in until either your answer was compelled, or you had died under it. This usage, so contrary to the humane spirit of our general institutions, has, I am happy to say, now been abrogated by statute. But the alternative provided for such a case is, in one point of view, even yet more serious."

The judge then proceeded to state the law as it then stood, but in regard to which a still further alteration has now taken place. At present, where a prisoner refuses to plead to an indictment, or "stands mute," as the technical term is, a plea of "not guilty" is entered on his behalf, and the trial goes on accordingly. But under the previous alteration, although the ancient barbarities of the *peine forte et dure* were abolished, the prisoner was still rigorously dealt by. The result of his persisting in "standing mute" was that the charge was taken as proved, and the consequences were the same as if the trial had taken place and a conviction ensued.

"So that in your case," the judge added, after having explained the above to Charles at length, "your refusal to plead, should you persist in it, will have the same effect as if this crime had been brought home to you by the evidence, and the jury had brought

in their verdict accordingly. In other words, you will
stand convicted of wilful murder. Are you prepared
for this ? "

"Yes," Charles answered ; quite steadily, but in
a dejected, almost humble tone.

"And you know the consequences ? " the judge
continued, his voice faltering with undisguised emotion
as he asked the question. "You know that you will
not only stand convicted of this—this most cruel and
deliberate murder, committed upon a child who could
never have wronged you, and who was your own near
connection ; stand as a felon in the dock where you
now are, proved upon your own admission to have
brought this heavy guilt upon yourself;—that you
must not only, I say, do this, but must also undergo
a felon's death ; be taken from the place where you
stand to that from which you came, and there be
executed as you know such criminals are executed ;—
a sentence of which I warn you there would not be
the faintest hope, in your case, of any commutation
being asked or granted :—you know, and are prepared
for all this ? "

"I am, my Lord," said Charles, still in the same
humble tone. The judge, who was a man of quick

sensibility, little impaired by the hardening influences of his profession, leant his face forwards for a minute or two in both his hands, unable longer to control his emotion. He was in fact grievously disappointed. Something in the prisoner's look and manner on entering the court, while it awakened in him the same sympathy which it had produced in the bystanders generally, had made the impression more permanent. He had entertained no doubt but that Charles would plead the ordinary plea of "not guilty;" and he was prepared to allow the fullest weight to any exculpatory evidence which might be advanced in reply to the charge; and which he had persuaded himself would be forthcoming, notwithstanding the strong grounds of presumption on which the latter rested.

The feeling thus exhibited by the person principally charged with the investigation of the case was re-sponded to by others present. More than one of the jurors, honest yeomen of the neighbourhood, might be seen, with strong weather-stained knuckles, dashing a tear out from under his eyelids.

This scene, so rare in a court of justice, was soon terminated, and the judge, resuming his ordinary calmness of demeanour, again looked at Charles with the same fixed scrutiny as before. He then leant his head on one hand, and thought intently for some little time longer.

"There is something I do not understand about this matter," he said at length, looking towards the bar-seats. "Is the prisoner defended by counsel?"

"I believe not, my Lord," replied the counsel for the prosecution.

"Indeed! That is another singular feature in a case like this. What legal assistance has this young man?"

Mr. Rigwell's clerk rose, and, bowing respectfully to the court, stated that his own services, as well as those of his employer, who had been for many years the professional adviser of the family, had been offered to the prisoner, but that he had peremptorily declined them. The speaker added that he had himself remained in court that morning to be of any assistance if required, but that the prisoner persisted in refusing to hold any communication with him.

"There is another charge to be dealt with, I believe," said the judge, "arising out of this deplorable business. This young gentleman's sister is charged, is she not?"

In reply, his Lordship was informed of the decision which the grand jury had come to in Helen's case.

Again the judge thought for a minute or two, in the same attitude as before. "I shall take the responsibility on myself," he at length said, addressing the counsel for the prosecution. "There is something which we have not got to the bottom of. I must take time to consider it; a few hours' delay at any rate will not prejudice the ends of justice. I shall not proceed further in this trial to-day. If any of the other Crown cases are ready they can be called on; if not, I will help my brother with the Nisi Prius list, which he tells me is a heavy one. At ten to-morrow morning I will take this case," continued the judge, addressing the counsel as before. "In the interval, I will endeavour to procure some information for my own guidance in it. It may be," he continued, turning to the High Sheriff, who was seated near him, and speaking in a low tone, "that you may have to empannel your jury for a different purpose to-morrow;—that of ascertaining the state of the prisoner's mind. I can detect no aberration myself; on the contrary, his manner is unusually

calm and self-possessed. But these very circumstances, coupled with his singular and persistent
refusal to plead, or to accept any assistance for his
defence, may be themselves the indicia of some delusion ;—something wrong, somewhere."

Meanwhile, the judge was not the only person
in court who had become impressed with this latter
conviction. One of the spectators, at any rate,
might have been seen, during the latter stage of
the proceedings, to have exhibited an agitation even
beyond what the trial would in any case have excited
in him. This was Mr. Latrobe.

Already, in many anxious musings, ever since
Helen's disclosure, the curate had begun to question
the correctness of his own conviction of Charles'
guilt. He had indeed promised Helen to dismiss
this belief from his mind altogether, and as far as
act and speech went, had religiously done so. But,
the persuasion itself, deep-seated as it had been,
was less easy to eradicate. Besides, even admitting
Mr. Fortescue's presence on the evening of Fred's
disappearance, it was most difficult to suggest any
motive for his having been concerned in such a
crime, or to understand in any way the time and

mode of its perpetration. Still, there he had been ;
and, to this extent, and even apart from the obliga-
tions of his own promise to Helen, Mr. Latrobe felt
that there was a new, and justifiable presumption in
Charles' favour. A presumption, he now thought,
sufficient to make it possible that the circumstances
which told against Charles himself might be explained.

In the course of the trial however Mr. Latrobe
had arrived at a conclusion far beyond this mere
argumentative result. Something in Charles' manner
had inspired him, even more powerfully than it had
the judge, with the suspicion of there being some
undetected mystery about the whole matter ; of
Charles being entirely and absolutely innocent :
with an intuition, finally, very vague and distant,
but still an intuition, of the real motives under which
the latter was at present acting !

Imperfectly developed as this conviction in
Mr. Latrobe's mind still was, it struck him with
a keen anguish. He marvelled at himself, hated
himself, for not having surmised it earlier.

" This must not go on," he said, starting to his
feet while the judge was occupied as above, and

speaking to Mr. Rigwell's clerk, who was still beside
him. "There is some fatal mistake about all this;
I am almost satisfied of it. I cannot bear it. I
must at once communicate to his Lordship what we
know about the matter: what Miss Armitage has
stated."

"You mean in regard to Mr. Fortescue," said
the clerk, to whom his employer had communicated
thus much in explanation of the inquiry he was
pressing.

"Yes, yes. It ought to be known: known at
once, to everybody. Good Heaven, how blind we
may all prove to have been!"

"Mr. Latrobe," said the clerk, earnestly, "you
will do your friend a serious mischief if you act
as you propose. It is exactly what Mr. Rigwell was
anxious to avoid, and with good reason. I quite
understand your excitement in the matter; in fact,
I share it myself; but it would be fatally impolitic
to disclose the circumstance now: there is no
possible necessity for it. The trial is adjourned
until to-morrow morning, and you may be satisfied
from the judge's manner, that whatever takes place
in the interval will be, if anything, for the prisoner's

advantage. Long before to-morrow, probably within an hour or two of the present time, Mr. Rigwell will be here with his proofs complete : the entire chain of evidence ready for production. To state this one unsupported fact at present would greatly impair the result. I give you my word of honour that it would injure our young friend's case most seriously."

Very reluctantly, Mr. Latrobe once more allowed himself to be persuaded. He might hardly have done so had he not recollected his promise to Mr. Rigwell not to prejudice the proofs he was collecting by any previous interference in the case, and felt bound to act upon it.

The judge retired soon after, and Charles was removed from the dock, in the custody of the police as before. Meanwhile however events had been in progress outside the court which produced an unforeseen effect upon the issue of the trial, and which it is now high time to detail.

CHAPTER XIV.

DURING the day or two preceding the assizes the county and town magistrates had received information of the possibility of some outbreak taking place on this occasion. The lower orders in the town, and even many of those of a grade above them, were, it was stated, greatly infuriated against Charles. It was the same feeling, in fact, which had so strongly manifested itself at Hastings on the day of his arrest, and which had rapidly extended to other parts of the county, and especially to Lewes, where the trial was to take place. And the excitement thus created, instead of experiencing any diminution in the interval, was found rather to have intensified.

This strong feeling against Charles was owing, as already stated, not merely to the atrocity of the crime for which he was arrested, but still more, and mainly, to the cowardice he was thought to have shown in remaining silent under Helen's committal, and thus exposing her to the consequences of his own act. When an English populace once becomes possessed with a sentiment of this kind, it transports them almost beyond the possibility of control. Words were hardly strong enough to express the indignation which was generally felt at such dastardly conduct. And from the information which had thus reached the authorities even before the commencement of the trial, it appeared that words were not the only result which was to be apprehended: the prisoner was openly threatened with personal violence. Even if a conviction were obtained, as no doubt was felt it would be, and the extreme penalty of the law inflicted, the punishment seemed inadequate to the offence. How far any actual combination existed to give effect to the feelings thus expressed was uncertain; but, premeditated or otherwise, there was an unquestionable risk of an attack being made upon Charles, and the magistrates were recommended to take steps accordingly.

With this view, besides largely reinforcing the ordinary police, a body of special constables had been

privately sworn in, so as to be ready to act on
emergency. Information had also been given at the
Brighton barracks that some assistance might be
required, and the officer in charge there had a small
body of mounted soldiers ready to be sent over to
Lewes at any moment.

These preparations for resisting actual force were
coupled with some obvious precautions for rendering
a resort to them unnecessary. To avoid attracting
the observation of the mob on the prisoner's way
from the Lewes gaol to the assize court, it had been
arranged that he should be brought to the latter at
the earliest possible hour of the morning, and there
detained until the trial was called on. This had
accordingly been done, and with as successful a result
as could have been wished. More than an hour
before daybreak, Charles had been roused from sleep
and placed in an ordinary hired carriage, the passage
of which through the streets was witnessed by few
persons, and those wholly unaware of what it contained. On reaching the court, Charles was confined,
strongly handcuffed, in a room on the basement of
the building. Some breakfast was here brought
him; and he continued to occupy this apartment

during the forenoon, and up to the time of his attendance being required in court. The handcuffs were then removed, and Charles placed in the dock; where the incidents had taken place which have been described in the last chapter.

Meanwhile the position of matters outside had, for some time past, become sufficiently threatening. Long before the usual hour of the court opening, the approaches to it had been crowded almost to the same extent as the building itself was by those who had been fortunate enough to procure admission. When the Sheriff and judges drove up, with some difficulty making their way, expectation was keenly roused, as it was supposed the police-van would follow. When this did not happen, the mob consoled themselves by the suggestion that probably Charles would not be sent for until the trial was called on. As the forenoon however wore away without the expected vehicle making its appearance, and a rumour from within the court, soon confirmed into a certainty, apprised those without that they had been cheated out of this part of the proceedings, and that the prisoner was actually in the dock, an evident, and alarming movement of menace took place.

"We'll do for him yet," was the cry which issued from more than one of the crowd.

It was some half-hour or so before this discovery on the part of the mob that a heavy-looking man, with the personal adornments of a swell of the first water, sauntered out of the court where he had been seated. Charles had not been placed in the dock at the time, and this person, apparently despairing of the *cause célèbre* coming on at present, lighted a cigar from his case; moving back as he did so from the street and pavement, which were densely thronged, to the further end of an archway opening from the latter. Here he planted himself against a door-post, and, with a hand in each pocket, began to puff away to his satisfaction.

He had been thus occupied for some minutes, when his eye fell on a policeman stationed a few yards from him, in a narrow alley into which the archway led, and who immediately touched his hat. The smoker, in whom the reader may or may not have recognized a certain Mr. Jarvis Jones mentioned in a previous volume, removed his cigar. "Hallo, Baynes," he said; "what brings you here? I thought you went to Brighton after you left our place."

"I did, sir," answered the man, who had formerly been a servant in Mr. Jones' family. "I am still on the police force there, but they've drafted thirty of us over here for the assizes."

"What; do they expect any row?" asked Mr. Jones.

"Rayther that, sir, and no mistake," was the man's answer. "I doubt if some of us won't have a bloody crown before the day's through."

"About this prisoner, I suppose; this young Armitage?" asked Mr. Jones, in whose mind the circumstances of his own encounter with Charles some months previously rankled with undiminished violence. He had in fact driven over to Lewes at an early hour that morning with the express object of gratifying the hatred which he thus nursed.

"The same, sir," replied the man, in answer to Mr. Jones' question. "It's an ugly case enough in itself; and likely to be uglier still for the young man if the crowd get their own way. They'd make short work with him enough. Their blood's a good deal up, some of them, at his having got here this morning without their finding it out. Some of our people, who ought to know, think he'll be got off on the trial, after all. I can't say as to that; but I hope these chaps outside won't get the same idea. If they once thought that, they'd go hard to burn the gaol, if they couldn't get him otherways."

"But if so, Baynes," asked Mr. Jones, "what's the use of your being here? You'll be wanted out in the main street, I should suppose."

"Well, sir," replied the man, "I don't mind telling you: of course, I shouldn't let everybody into the secret. The fact is, it's a bit of sharp practice they've got: it was our superintendent at Brighton as put them up to it. As soon as the prisoner's trial's over, he will be moved out through this bit of a lane. We're on duty here, I and another constable at the further end, to prevent any one coming along it; although there's not much fear of that: it only leads to some gardens and the like."

"Oh! indeed," said Mr. Jones. "Have a cigar, Baynes: you'll be glad of it when you're off work by-and-by. I should like to hear about this manœuvre of yours: it sounds clever."

"Thank'ee, sir," said the man, touching his hat again as he accepted the proffered bribe. "Well, the plan they've got settled is just this. When the trial's gone on a bit, they'll have the regular police-van brought up the main street here, in front of the courts, with the sergeant and a strongish lot of our men to make way for it as they best can ; although I don't expect much difficulty about that : they'll let the van come up to the Court easily enough."

" Who do you mean by ' they ? ' " asked Mr. Jones, taking out of his mouth the cigar, to the discussion of which he had returned, and replacing it with an indifferent air as his companion answered.

" I mean the ringleaders, sir," the man replied. " It's been a regular concerted thing, we hear. There's a chap with a cock eye and a wooden leg is at the bottom of it. But as I was a saying, they'll let the van come through without much trouble ; in fact, that'll be their game : they'll make sure of getting him then. But they'll miss their bird, for all that."

" Ah ! I see," said Mr. Jones. " The van, with the sergeant and police, will stand in front of the Court as a make-believe ; and meanwhile the prisoner will be got out down this lane here. How will that be done, by the way ? "

" Nothing easier, sir. Next door to the Courts

there's a house which has a door into them, and
another into the lane ;—a man lives there who takes
care of the place when there's no 'sizes or sessions
being held ;—and at the lower end of the lane he'll be
took through a house into another street, ever so far
from what's going on. There they'll have a light cart
at the door, driven by one of our men in plain
clothes, and with a lot of straw in the bottom of it.
They'll stow him in under the straw; and another
constable, in plain clothes too, will jump up in the
cart to look after him. Then they'll drive right out
of the town for some distance, and come back into it
by the old Hastings road, leading up by the far side
of the gaol, where nobody would ever think of
coming. There's a side entrance there at which he
could be took in."

"Ah! I see," said Mr. Jones. "And so, while
the mob are eating their heads off in front here, the
prisoner will be safe and snug in the gaol?"

"That's about it, sir," said the man.

"Well, good-day, Baynes. I hope you won't get
your head broke; but there's some chance of it. I'll
go back into court now." And, throwing away the
end of his cigar, the speaker turned out of the passage.

As he did so, a very ominous smile passed for an instant over his fat puffy cheeks. " So they'll let him off, will they ? " he muttered to himself. " I think I'll try what I can do then."

Mr. Jones had now passed from the archway into the main street, but he made no attempt to get back into court; on the contrary, he walked down the street in the direction in which the gaol lay, making his way leisurely in and out of the densely thronged masses by whom it was occupied. As he did so, the police-van with its escort drove up, and, as the policeman had anticipated, was allowed to reach the front of the Court without further obstruction than arose from the necessity of displacing its own width of the crowd in passing ; the severed portions of which immediately closed in behind it, as a fluid substance might have done. Although Mr. Jones showed no particular hurry in his movements, he was evidently keeping a vigilant look-out for some person whom he wished to see; and, coming to a flight of steps leading up to a house, contrived to get a footing for a minute or two on the uppermost, the better to conduct his scrutiny.

The latter soon proved successful. A short

distance down the street, on the opposite side of
the way, stood a man whose amputated leg, and a
squint which added a sinister expression to features
far from prepossessing in themselves, easily identified
him as the ringleader of whom the policeman had
spoken. Mr. Jones at once quitted his post of
observation, and, making his way across the street
with some trouble, succeeded eventually in getting
next to this person; although his movements had
been made in such a leisurely and indifferent manner
as to appear the result of accident. "Cleverish
dodge too," Mr. Jones said, after he had stood for a
minute, and as if speaking to himself; "really, very
good indeed : shouldn't have thought they'd have
been up to it down here."

"What's that, guv'nor?" said the man next him,
on whom Mr. Jones saw by a quick glance that
his words had produced a powerful impression.
"Wot's the dodge?"

Mr. Jones affected to start, and look around at
his neighbour. "What's that to you, my friend?"
he asked after a short scrutiny.

"'Tain't no more to me than to any one else,
as I knows of," said the man gruffly. "Only I

wanted to know wot's a dodge, and who'r'n up to it."

"Well, I'll tell you if you like; you seem an honest fellow enough. I meant that police-van there."

"And where's the dodge in that, guv'nor?"

"What do you suppose it's there for?" asked Mr. Jones.

"There for? why to take that blackguard young chap back to gaol, ain't it?" said the man.

"No, it ain't," replied Mr. Jones. "He won't see the inside of that machine to-day. Most likely he'll be let off altogether; but, at any rate, they won't take him back to the gaol that way: they're not so green."

"How will he be took then?" asked the man.

Mr. Jones again looked at the speaker. "Tell me why you want to know, and I'll tell you how," he said. "That's fair-play, isn't it?"

"You knows how it's to be done?" asked the man, suspiciously.

"Yes."

"As you're a gentleman?"

"Upon my honour as a gentleman."

"Well then, sir," the man said, touching his hat

for the first time, " there's a few of us here that 'ud like to get hold of the prisoner ; that's all. He'd be the better for having a little taste of English law, as we administers it : they'll be letting him off too easy in there, I expect."

" Ah ! I see," said Mr. Jones. " Well, I don't say you're wrong. It was a horrible business from first to last ; and that about the sister was the worst of all. He's a black-hearted young villain, that's the fact. You want to duck him, I suppose, or something of that sort ? "

" Something of that sort," said the man, with a sneer which gave him a more dangerous expression than ever.

" Well, if you're really in earnest," said Mr. Jones, " I'll give you the hint, as I promised. You couldn't find a needle in a bottle of hay, I suppose, could you ? "

" No, I couldn't," said the man, surlily.

" Nor in a cart half-full of straw, perhaps," continued Mr. Jones.

" No, I couldn't," the other again answered. " What are you going and making a fool of a fellow for ? "

"But if there was a man lying at the bottom of a cart among a lot of straw perhaps you could find him?"

Mr. Jones' companion looked up at him with a quick glance of intelligence. "And where did we ought to go for that 'ere, sir," he asked.

"Well, of course I don't know exactly; "I think, if it were my business, that, as the gaol is the place he is to be taken to, I should keep a look-out near the gaol. And if the gaol had two entrances, I don't think I should look out near the public one: at least, I shouldn't keep the principal look-out there."

"I begins to trust you, guv'nor," said the man, who had been watching Mr. Jones in his turn. "I see's you've no liking for the young chap yourself: I see'd it in your eye just then. Yes, there is two entrances, as you calls it: there's a side one, in the Foregate, where the coach road used to go. Daresay now a few of us might happen to be down that way, by-and-by. Won't give up the van, though, neither; will us?" the man continued, with a sudden return of suspicion. "Maybe you're only in the pay of some of them; although, hang it all, you do look as if you

meant business. We'll have some picked fellows
down to the gaol, and leave the rest up in the street
here, to settle the van, if he should come this 'ere
way: they're muffs, many of them, but they'd be
up to that. Thank'ee, guv'nor, good afternoon."
And the owner of the wooden leg stumped away to
make his preparations.

*　　*　　*　　*　　*　　*

It was some hour or two after the conversation
just detailed, that a man in a fisherman's dress,
looking hot and jaded, arrived in the vicinity of
Lewes. He had followed the road which led from
Hastings to that place, and on approaching the
latter, paused for a minute where it forked about
half a mile from the town; the more frequented track
making a circuit round a rising ground, while the
other, now evidently little used, struck directly up
the ascent. The day was a sultry one, such as often
occurs in early spring, and the dusty look of the
main road determined the pedestrian, whom the
reader will easily surmise to have been Ralph, to
follow that which mounted the hill.

Ralph had left home at an exceedingly early hour
that morning, and had made no doubt of being in

ample time for the trial. But his powers as a walker
had been imperfectly cultivated; and even before he
reached Bexhill he had begun to think this mode of
progression a detestable exchange for that of his own
boat. He persevered however with the constancy of
a martyr; and after undergoing untold hardship,
actually came in sight of Lewes at last: many hours
later than he had intended, but still before the afternoon had sensibly declined.

As Ralph ascended the hill, he began to repent of
his choice of road, which told with peculiar severity
at the end of his walk. It was some time in consequence before he found himself at the top; and when
he at length did so, he was fain to sit down on a
bank by the side of the road, unfasten his waistcoat
and neck-handkerchief, and recover some amount of
breath before proceeding.

While thus engaged, Ralph heard wheels coming
up the hill which he had just surmounted; shortly
afterwards, a cart containing two men, one driving
and the other seated on the flat board at the side,
passed him at a rapid trot, and proceeded at full speed
into the town.

The nearest building in the latter, and which in

fact lay immediately at Ralph's feet as he sat on the bank, was an unpromising flint and stone edifice, en-closed on all sides by a wall surmounted with *chevaux de frise*, in which he had no difficulty in recognizing the county gaol. As the cart approached this, it began to slacken its speed; at the same moment, a door in the enclosing wall was thrown open, and a couple of warders appeared at the entrance, evidently waiting for the cart to draw up there.

Its arrival however was frustrated. Between the foot of the hill and the door were two or three hundred yards of flat ground, terminating in the Fore-gate already mentioned; a narrow street of scattered houses which formed the commencement of the town on this side. On the left of this flat, nearly opposite to the gaol, ran a long line of wooden sheds, present-ing the appearance of a rope walk, although now evidently disused. When the cart reached the flat piece, its occupants, and the two warders at the gate, were the only persons visible, either on the road or in the street beyond; but as the pace of the vehicle slackened, the number of actors in the scene received an addition equally unexpected and unwelcome. Some eight or nine men, dressed uniformly in

smock-frocks and with crape tied over the lower part
of their faces, emerged from the rope walk at full
speed, and threw themselves upon the cart; two of
them standing at the horse's head, while the
remainder attacked the driver and his companion.

The gaol-warders meanwhile had not been idle;
one of them hastily sprang his rattle, and the two
then ran to the assistance of the men in the cart.
They were too late however. The vehicle was at
some distance from the gate, and before they could
reach it, the driver and the man with him, who were
wholly unprepared for such an occurrence, were over-
mastered and their arms tied behind them. The
assailants then tossed out some straw from the cart,
and finally lifted from it some person, tightly handcuffed; and in whom Ralph, before whose eyes the scene
just described had passed with the rapidity of a dream,
recognized, to his intense surprise, Charles Armitage.

Ralph's first emotions were those of considerable
satisfaction: he made no doubt that there was a
rescue going on; and, hurrying down the hill at his
best pace, prepared to take part in it. In the interval,
however, the men who had removed Charles from the
cart began to handle him in a way which showed that

their intention was anything but friendly. For a few
yards, two of them carried him between them ; finding that he struggled, although the handcuffs prevented his making any effectual resistance, they then
lowered him from their arms, and dragged him along
the road by the feet, in the direction of the town.

The object of this assault now became evident
enough. Rapidly as it had taken place, it had
already been communicated, doubtless by some concerted signal, to the mob in the main street, which
was at no great distance. The news quickly spread ;
and those who had been waiting in front of the
courts, wearied with their long detention, and doubly
incensed at the trick which had thus been again
played them, hurried pell-mell in the direction of the
conflict. Scattered parties of them were already seen
at the upper end of· the Foregate, which a short time
before had been so deserted, running towards the
spot at full speed, and evidently in sympathy with
Charles' captors. The latter on their part made the
best of their way to meet them, and in a minute or
two more would have effected their object.

The above position, which it has required some
lines to describe, Ralph took in at a glance. Hurry-

ing by the cart, where a sharp fight was now going on
between the rest of the assailants and the two gaol
officers, with some others whom the warder's rattle
had brought to their assistance, Ralph quickly caught
up with the two men who were dragging Charles.
His onset was unexpected, and a blow from the butt-
end of a stout walking-stick which the fisherman
carried laid one of the men prostrate on the ground,
stunned and bleeding ; the other dropped Charles,
and turning on Ralph struggled with him des-
perately, but unsuccessfully. After a short encounter
he too was thrown heavily to the ground, badly hurt. ₅
Ralph had now time to lift Charles, who had fainted
from the violence to which he had been subjected,
and carry him to the side of the road ; where he
remained, partly supported against a tree, but still
unconscious.

In the meantime however the mob were upon
them : those most in advance were within thirty
yards of the spot. Behind, the infuriated populace
poured into the narrow street in hundreds, choking it
up as they had done the main street previously.
Ralph however stood his ground ; he had placed
himself immediately in front of Charles, and now

flourished over his head the stout sapling which had already proved so useful. "The first on ye as comes for to touch him I'll brain with this stick," he said, determinedly.

As it appeared likely that Ralph would keep his word, the crowd hung back for some little time, in spite of their numbers. Where the first assailant must suffer, no one cares to be the first, however many may be coming afterwards; and the principle operates with special force where a mob is the attacking party. The respite however was of brief duration.

" 'Eave summat 'ard at 'em !" cried a voice some two or three ranks in the rear, and which in fact proceeded from the man with the wooden leg, with whom Mr. Jarvis Jones had conversed that morning.

This suggestion was at once acted upon. The pitching of the street was taken up, and afforded a supply of handy and dangerous missiles, which were freely thrown. In spite of Ralph's care, who stood before and protected him to the utmost of his power, Charles was struck two or three times. Ralph himself received a perfect volley; not a very well directed one, fortunately, or the consequences would have been fatal. As it was, the position had become untenable; and the crowd, no longer overawed by Ralph's posture of defence, were rapidly closing in upon them.

But the minute or two thus gained produced an important effect on the issue of the contest. During the interval, the warders from the gaol had not only overpowered those opposed to them, and released their own two men, but had received an important reinforce-ment of police and special constables; the news of the attack upon Charles having reached the town authorities almost as quickly as it had the mob. Thus strengthened, the defenders presented a compact and formidable force; they at once marched up the street, just in time to save Charles and his gallant protector, who were on the point of being surrounded. The former was still insensible; but there was no time to attend to him, as the mob, although they at first retired before the police for some distance, showed no symptoms of abandoning their object. Stones were again thrown; and although the police used their staves freely, and contested every inch of ground, they were gradually borne back by the weight of numbers. Charles' capture was again imminent.

It was at this critical juncture that the tramp of a body of horse became audible in the rear of the conflict; and nearly at the same moment, to the unspeakable relief of those who were maintaining it on such unequal terms, one or two cavalry uniforms were seen on the brow of the hill above the gaol.

This new arrival was due to a message from the Lewes authorities, despatched to Brighton at an earlier hour the same afternoon, requesting that the military might be forwarded without loss of time; the men were soon in the saddle, and rode over to Lewes at a round trot. Before they reached it, however, the attack upon Charles had taken place; and the magistrates, having been apprised of this, sent instructions for them to make a *détour* which would bring them in on the other side of the town. This was done, and they appeared on the scene of action as above described.

This opportune arrival soon changed the posture of affairs. The men seeing what was going on, galloped down the hill, and then formed at the bottom for a charge; the police opening their line to allow of their passage. For a moment or two the mob seemed disposed to stand their ground; but the sight of the horses close upon them made them think better of it. A few blows were struck with the flats of the sabres; but they were hardly necessary: seized with a panic proportioned to their previous violence, the rioters turned and fled in every direction; not only arresting the advance of those behind, who were still ignorant of the approach of the soldiers, but bearing them back with them in their retreat.

In a few minutes the street was comparatively clear: although more than one person in the crowd had been injured by the violence with which they had been forced back, and had to be supported or carried to their homes. Among those worst hurt, as the reader may probably be satisfied to learn, was Mr. Jarvis Jones. Although afraid of showing himself in the front, his anxiety to witness the success of his scheme had induced him to follow the crowd down the street; in their recoil, Mr. Jones lost his balance, and was literally trampled under foot by the fugitives; receiving injuries on the occasion which, it may be stated in anticipation, terminated his career a few weeks afterwards.

Meanwhile Charles, who still continued insensible,

and was bleeding from a wound in the temple, had
been at last lifted from the spot where Ralph had
placed him, and carried into the gaol: not to his
previous place of confinement there, but to a bedroom
on an upper floor which was temporarily appropriated
for his use. A surgeon was at once sent for, and
arrived shortly afterwards, accompanied by Mr.
Latrobe; who had received the intelligence nearly
at the same moment, and hastened to the spot.

By the time they entered Charles' room, he had
regained consciousness, and was sitting up on the
bed; the blood still streaming from his forehead, but
apparently not seriously hurt. He evinced so much
agitation, however, at the sight of Mr. Latrobe that
the surgeon interfered.

" I must be left quite alone," he said.   " If you
will wait downstairs for a few minutes, I will promise
you to come and report."

Mr. Latrobe obeyed, and the surgeon at once
proceeded to examine the wound. He was as good
as his word, and joined Mr. Latrobe in the lobby of
the gaol shortly afterwards.

" As far as can be seen," he said, " there is no
cause for apprehension; the cut on the temple is

nothing, and there is no other external injury visible.
I confess however there is something I do not like
about the look of the eye : he was dragged for some
distance, I am told, before he could be rescued ; and
I am not satisfied that some injury on the brain
has not been sustained."

" Would that be likely to be serious?" Mr. Latrobe
asked.

The surgeon shrugged his shoulders. " No saying, my good sir: I shall be able to judge better
in half-an-hour or so. At present the young man
seems tolerably himself; quite so, in fact: he is
still sitting up, and appears to treat the matter very
lightly. As you are interested in him, I hope it
is all right."

" But does not this show there is no serious
mischief?" asked Mr. Latrobe. " He could not be so
free from uneasiness if there were."

" That does not at all follow," replied the
surgeon. " Of the two, I had rather that there was
more uneasiness :—it would be an indication that we
knew the worst of it. As it is, he may keep comparatively well for some hours, and then effusion take
place in a moment. However, I will make a still

more thorough examination, if you will do an errand for me."

" With pleasure ; what is it ? "

" To call at my surgery in the High Street, nearly opposite the hotel, and tell the assistant to come down at once. He should bring with him the case of instruments in the left corner drawer of my writing-table. Do not come back yourself," the surgeon added, as Mr. Latrobe was leaving the room : " it will be better for your friend at present that he should not think you are here ; and I will bring you a further report at the hotel. I must go back home in any case for half-an-hour or so, and I will come over to you there. Will you be in the coffee-room ? "

" No ; we have a private sitting-room : it is engaged in the name of Mr. Rigwell, who is the solicitor for the prisoner's defence."

" Very well," said the surgeon : " I will ask for that name. You may expect me in an hour at furthest."

Mr. Latrobe executed his commission, and then, having ascertained that Helen's removal from the Court had been effected without disturbance, returned

to the room at the hotel of which he had spoken, and
sat anxiously awaiting the surgeon's appearance.
Mr. Rigwell's managing clerk, with two or three
other gentlemen who were interested in the case
as friends of the late Mr. Armitage, were also in
the room.

A good deal more than an hour elapsed before
the expected visitor made his appearance; when he
at length did so, it was evident that he brought bad
news. Mr. Latrobe started from his seat as he read
the expression on the surgeon's face.

"You think there is danger?" he asked falteringly.

"There is no near relative of the young man's in
the room, I suppose?" the surgeon asked in reply,
speaking aside to Mr. Latrobe.

"None," Mr. Latrobe answered.

"Then," the surgeon continued aloud, "I need
not hesitate to tell you the worst. The case is quite
hopeless. As I have already said, the external
wound is nothing; but I have ascertained that there
is a fatal internal injury,—quite confirming the
unsatisfactory appearance in the eye, with which I
was struck on first seeing him. He is still, to
outward appearance, much as when you left him;

but the laceration in the brain is making steady progress, and effusion must take place inevitably in a few hours. He cannot last out the night : probably it will be still earlier."

The curate wrung his hands in bitter grief. " Can nothing be done ? " he asked, vehemently.

" Nothing," was the reply : " absolutely nothing. I will be there of course ; for part of the time at any rate : but I am quite powerless."

" I may go to him now ? " inquired Mr. Latrobe eagerly. " And his sister too ; she is confined in the same building, on this charge : surely they will allow her to see him."

" Unquestionably, I should think," answered the surgeon. " As regards my own department, there is no reason whatever why you should not go, both of you ; it can make no possible difference, I grieve to say : and your being there will probably now not even excite him as it did before. He is perceptibly calmer ; the first symptom of coma supervening. In these cases, the fatal result usually takes place after the lapse of several hours, and with great suddenness ; but here it will be more gradual, and, to that extent, less painful to witness. He will most likely

be able to converse for some time longer, and seem
much as usual, although a medical eye could detect
what is going on. The coma, or lethargy, will then
become apparent; he will grow drowsy, and finally
unconscious, and will pass away in that state : I
imagine with little suffering. If you like to go now
you can, and I will be back there presently."

Mr. Latrobe seized his hat, and was about to
quit the room, when he was unexpectedly detained.
His conversation with the surgeon had so absorbed
him and the other gentlemen present, that they had
not heard a chaise drive rapidly up to the hotel door.
The occupant of it stepped out at once, taking with
him a large bag of papers ; he mounted the stairs of
the hotel, three at a time, and entering the room
without knocking, showed to those present the face
and figure of Mr. Rigwell, now labouring under an
excess of pleasurable excitement.

"Eureka !" he cried, without pausing to take
breath. "Everything as clear as crystal. Got the
finishing link at last, thank goodness. Though, only
think of its not having turned up before :—would
have saved us all the trouble."

"I am sorry to say—" Mr. Latrobe began.

" Sorry ! " interrupted the attorney vivaciously :
" don't be sorry for anything. Look here," he
continued, " we've found some one who saw him,
Mr. Fortescue, actually in Hastings itself : that's
why I'm so late. My part of the work, as much of
it as was left, was all finished off at Ticehurst this
morning ; and I was just starting for this place, when
I got an express from Hastings to tell me of this
discovery. It was a woman who keeps a small
eating-house, or coffee-shop, or something of the
kind, between the beach and George Street. Identified the party at once ; drew a verbal picture of
him to the life from her own memory, without our
men prompting her the least. And in a boatman's
dress too, just as . . . . But hallo ! though ; what
is the matter ? You don't seem to think anything
of it."

" You are too late, Mr. Rigwell," said one of the
gentlemen present, very gravely.

" Too late ! Oh ! dear no ! It can be put
straight with the greatest ease, whatever has
happened."

" There are some things which can never be put
straight in this world," replied the same speaker.

" Did you see or hear nothing unusual as you came up .
the street ? "

"Not I: I was leaning back in the chaise,
reading up some of the points in the case. But,
good heaven, what is it: what can have happened?"
added the attorney, in whose kind-hearted nature the
triumph of success had already given way to an agony
of dismay and apprehension.

In a few hurried words, the person who had
already spoken informed Mr. Rigwell; who stood
grasping the back of a chair during the narration of
the catastrophe which had taken place. Very
bitterly, when the recital was concluded, did the
attorney lament the time which his search had occupied ; the detention caused by his *détour* to Hastings
that morning : even the skill and industry which
had at length succeeded in effecting his object. Loud
was his self-accusation, at one time for having
undertaken to prosecute the inquiry at all, at
another for not having conducted it to an earlier
close. Alas ! as his informant had said, it *was*
too late !

Mr. Latrobe, after a warm and sympathizing
pressure of the worthy lawyer's hand, had started a

second time to leave the room, when he was again interrupted.

On this occasion the reader is acquainted with the cause.

The necessary recapitulation of the last few chapters has now brought my story to a point in which the narrator re-appears as a personal actor in its scenes.

The post-chaise in which I had driven from Hastings this afternoon had followed close upon Mr. Rigwell's, and reached the door of the Lewes hotel not more than a quarter-of-an-hour after he had alighted there.

CHAPTER XV.

THE swooning fit which had attacked me on entering the hotel was not of long duration. While it lasted, I had been removed into a ground-floor sitting-room, and placed on the sofa. On my recovering consciousness, the first person on whom my eye fell was Mr. Latrobe. The news of the arrival of a stranger, who purported to be the bearer of evidence in Charles's favour, spread rapidly through the various parties collected in the hotel, and indeed through the town generally: having reached Mr. Latrobe's ears, he was impelled, anxious as he was to see Charles, to ascertain the truth of the report.

A surgeon had been fetched for me on my swooning,—the same who had been summoned for Charles, —and Mr. Latrobe, Mr. Rigwell, and one or two others accompanied him. Mr. Latrobe's surprise on

seeing me was unbounded. I was still unconscious;
but the surgeon assured him I was suffering only
from exhaustion, and should probably recover in a
few minutes; and he waited accordingly. His face,
as I have said, was the first I saw when the attack
left me and I was able to sit up. I seemed to feel
no wonder at his being there : I felt nothing ; thought
of nothing, but my one object.

"Is the trial over ? " I exclaimed, as I had
already done on first entering the hotel.

" The trial ? " Mr. Latrobe asked, almost
absently. So much had subsequent occurrences
effaced the recollection even of that morning's
proceedings.

"Yes : yes. You know what I would say.
The trial; his trial. Answer me," I exclaimed
vehemently.

"No, it is not over," said the curate; echoing in
his turn the utterances of those whom I had first
met at the inn-door.

"Thank Heaven for that at least," I cried. "Mr.
Latrobe," I continued, "I do not know what coinci-
dence has brought you here : or rather, of course,
I do know ; but it is a most fortunate circumstance.

I must speak with you instantly; and alone : quite
alone."

The surgeon here interposed. "My dear young
lady," he said kindly, "you shall do all that you
wish in a few minutes; but I peremptorily forbid
your speaking further until you have had some
refreshment : you are greatly and obviously exhausted, and will break down again. I am quite
satisfied these gentlemen will second me."

I was compelled to gulp down a glass of wine,
into which I crumbled a few morsels of biscuit.
Then, at last, I was free. All present, excepting
Mr. Latrobe, withdrew. I was left alone with God's
minister : with the man whose advice I had asked—
and rejected.

"Mr. Latrobe," I said, when the door had closed
behind the last departure, "I have something most
important to communicate : something which is very
terrible for me to tell, and for you to hear; but I
can bear more than that for his sake. Mr. Latrobe,"
I cried, starting up from my seat as something
in his expression struck me, "why do you look
like that? Is anything wrong? I remember those
people at the entrance said something : is any-

thing wrong?" I cried, vehemently. "Is he safe?
Is he?"

"Charles Armitage?"

"Of course I mean him. What has happened,
Mr. Latrobe? Is he dead? For the love of heaven,
of our common faith, tell me."

"He lives, Miss Secretan," answered the Curate,
very sadly; calling me, in his grief, by my old
name. "But the sands of life are running short
now. The medical gentleman whom you saw here
just now informs me that he cannot live through
the night. He was attacked by the mob on his way
from the Court this morning: cruelly and shamefully
attacked: injured in the head somewhere. The
cowardly murderers!"

"Murderers!" I echoed sarcastically; for the
iron was eating into me to the quick. "Have you
ever seen one, when you call them that name? Look
at me and you will know better, Mr. Latrobe. I am
his murderer! Look at this bauble here," and I
tore from my wrist a bracelet which I had on the
day I left Switzerland and had since forgotten:
"look at this. It is part of the hire for it. Oh!
Charles, Charles!"

His name awakened some softer feeling, and I think saved my reason; which was tottering with the exhaustion of the last few days, and with the terrible news I had just heard. I leant on the sofa: not weeping, my heart was too hot for that; but uttering a low kind of cry.

Mr. Latrobe's manner had been stern and reserved during the previous conversation, but my evident distress softened him. "Mrs. Fortescue," he said gently, "it is imperative that I should go down to Charles as quickly as possible. If what you wish to tell me can tend in any way to relieve him from this most cruel imputation, I will gladly wait and listen to it; but let me intreat you, for all our sakes, to calm yourself: the moments are very precious. I should add," continued the curate after a short pause, "that I am already acquainted, or probably so, with part of your story. Mr. Fortescue has been tracked from your house to Hastings; and his presence here on that unhappy night, in a disguise and under circumstances which make it almost impossible that he should not have been connected with the child's murder, are fully established. What his object can have been, or why you now charge yourself,

in the vehement terms you do, with this further guilt
of Charles's death, I cannot form the faintest conception."

. Time precious! Ah! but it was! To whom so
more than to me?

The wine had given me force. I seated myself
again on the sofa, and determined that voice and
tongue should do my bidding. And then I told
Mr. Latrobe everything, from first to last.

Everything, without cloak or reservation, that
could evidence Charles's innocence or my own guilt :
everything; excepting that one secret only of my
love. And that was not a secret much longer.

Just as I spoke, just so did Mr. Latrobe listen.
I spoke, as I might have read out from a scientific
treatise, without changing tone or posture ; and he
listened, patiently and uninterruptingly.

" I have one thing to ask," I said, " before
concluding. Of Charles's arrest I had heard, as I
told you, in Switzerland ; its results I have learnt
from yourself this evening. But I have not heard—I
cannot possibly divine — the reason of his being
arrested. What was it ? "

And then my heart, bleeding and scarred as it

already was, received the last blow. Then I learnt the results of my innocent but most fatal theft at Hastings. Then I identified the handkerchief, which I had taken up when Charles left it in the fisherman's cottage; had so long worn nearest to my heart; had, in a casual oversight, left on my dressing-table at Dalemain :—identified this with the one which Mr. Fortescue, as he told me in his letter at the time, took with him to Cumberland. This then he still had with him at Hastings. With this he had staunched the child's blood on the night of his unwitting homicide. This had lain hidden beneath the stone ; until it appeared, an irrefragable but most lying witness, against the life of the only being I had ever loved. And this was my act !

A murderess doubly-dyed !

I told him this too : even this. And then I started to my feet. " I must be forgiven, Mr. Latrobe," I cried hoarsely. " I cannot bear it. He lives ; he comprehends : you tell me he does. He must hear all from you, and you must bring me his forgiveness. Mr. Latrobe, you are a priest ; a minister of the Gospel : you will not refuse me this ? "

Mr. Latrobe did not reply for a minute or two. He seemed almost stupefied with my narrative; hardly able to take in what I was asking so passionately.

"I pity you from the depth of my heart," he said at length. "Your penitence seems genuine, and I will gladly assist you, as far as lies in my power, to obtain that forgiveness from Heaven which is not denied to the most erring. I hardly know whether my duty ought to carry me beyond this, under present circumstances."

"It ought, it ought," I cried. "Heaven's pardon shall be sought, if prayer and self-abasement can win it. But I must have human forgiveness too: his forgiveness. Mr. Latrobe, will you not help me to get this?"

"I can see what state Charles is in," the curate said, half to himself, after a moment's thought. "Mrs. Fortescue," he then continued, addressing me, "I will repeat to him the substance of what you have told me, at any rate: assuming, that is, that he is in a condition to allow of my doing so; and I will faithfully report to you what he says in reply. Not to-night, however: not until everything is over.

I will not leave the gaol again," he added, averting his face, " until that happens ; but I will come up to you here as soon as possible afterwards."

" Here ! " I echoed. " Here ! You propose to leave me here, Mr. Latrobe ? "

" Surely yes. What can you do better ? "

" Remain here ! " I again exclaimed. " And with Charles dying a few streets off ! I will not do it, Mr. Latrobe : I must go with you. I do not ask to see him, to hear his voice again : Heaven knows how little worthy I am of that ; but under the same roof with him I must and will be."

" I cannot at all see the use of that, Mrs. Fortescue," the curate replied, somewhat coldly. " Surely after what you have just told me, you might be satisfied if I bring you, as I hope to do, the forgiveness of those whom you have so cruelly injured. " Excuse me," he added, rising and moving towards the door, "time is of the utmost consequence : I will leave you now, and return as I promised."

My heart was wrung to the quick by his chilling manner ; I could not bear it : the buried secret of my life leapt from me.

" Man ! " I cried, " I will not be put off: I *will* go there. I tell you I love him : I love him ! I have loved him always. Loved him from the first hour that I set foot in Hastings. Loved him when I contracted that accursed marriage. Love him now: oh ! how devotedly, how passionately ! Man ! I must—I will go there. You dare not say me nay."

He paused, overborne by my vehemence. Seeing this, I threw myself at his feet. " Mr. Latrobe," I said, " you cannot refuse me this. You have loved, yourself, as I know : will do so again ; for I feel there is a new hope dawning for you. But you can never love as I do : the happy never can know the love of despair. Mr. Latrobe, say that I may accompany you ! "

And then I prevailed. " Are you strong enough to walk with me down the street ? " he asked.

" Oh ! yes, yes. Hasten, Mr. Latrobe ; only let us start."

CHAPTER XVI.

THE afternoon on which so many important events
had occurred had been cloudy, but it was succeeded
by a bright clear evening. The moon, now approaching the full, shone overhead; a light air which
stirred the foliage of some gardens adjoining the
road, after we quitted the main street, bore with it a
fragrance redolent of the early spring.

The scene was one of quiet serenity; and the
homely little town, so lately disturbed by violence,
had now resumed an aspect in harmony with it. As
frequently happens, the effect of the attack upon the
prisoner had been to turn the feelings of the populace
in a wholly opposite direction. The news of the
severe and probably fatal injury which Charles had
received spread rapidly; and those who had been
foremost in their desire for inflicting upon him some

signal chastisement, now either laboured to conceal their own share in the transaction, or took a prominent part in denouncing it.

The revulsion of feeling thus caused was greatly increased, when it began to be rumoured that evidence was forthcoming which clearly established the prisoner's innocence. Mr. Rigwell's arrival, followed so soon afterwards by my own, caused a marked sensation, and formed the subject of numerous reports, more or less incorrect in detail, but all agreeing in the material fact. The person then, who had been the object of such unmeasured indignation a few hours previously, would prove, after all, to have been wrongly charged throughout!

The utmost grief was now expressed at this unhappy error. For an hour or two, repeated inquiries were made at the gaol; and knots of talkers, collected in the street or on the pavement, discussed the occurrence with a thoughtful and somewhat abashed air. As nothing could be done however, these gradually dropped off; and by the hour of which I am writing the streets were even more deserted than usual; their only occupants being an occasional constable on duty, or some townsman

returning homewards from canvassing the events of
the day at a neighbour's house.

The distance to the gaol was not great; but as
we walked, every limb was trembling under me.
Mr. Latrobe lent me his arm, and we proceeded
down the street together in silence; passed the
scene of the attack on Charles; reached the
building itself.

The casualty which had occurred that afternoon
had relaxed the rules of discipline in favour of those
connected with the prisoner, and Mr. Latrobe found
no difficulty in procuring admission for both of us.
A parlour was kindly placed at our service, and there
Mr. Latrobe left me; promising at once to communicate with Charles, if he should prove equal to
it, and to return and tell me the result. Helen, we
found, had been also allowed to visit her brother,
and was now in the room with him. The medical
attendant had come down again after seeing Mr.
Latrobe, but was now absent: he would return in
an hour or two.

I waited alone in the parlour. An extreme
stillness pervaded the whole place: the ticking of a
small clock on the mantelpiece; the occasional

dropping of a cinder from the fire which burned in the grate; once or twice, the scarcely audible closing of a door in some remote part of the building: no other sounds to break the silence.

And yet not a horror of stillness, such as the place might naturally have suggested; such as was consonant to my own errand there; to the guilt I had confessed, the life-long penalty I was to bear: it was rather a peaceful, Sabbath-like hush. So peaceful, that, in spite of myself, it woke up me in some childish memory or the other of a Sunday spent in the country years ago, with the bells chiming over the corn-fields, and the labourers passing with bowed head under the church-porch. My eyes filled with tears; the first that I had shed since quitting Switzerland, or, in fact, for many a long week before: the first, when I came to think of it, since he and I had stood together in Ralph's cottage !

Then, at last, the door was gently opened. I expected Mr. Latrobe, but saw Helen.

For one second, the old hard feeling, the old hate, offspring of my own evil doing, stirred bitterly within me. For one second only. Then I cast away from me for ever all pride and ruthlessness, and humbled myself at the feet of her whom I had wronged.

"Do not do that, Maria," said Helen; "I have come to bring you his forgiveness."

"And yours?" I asked, still without changing my posture. "You cannot do it, Helen!"

"Oh! yes, yes," Helen exclaimed. "Do not doubt it. Show that you do not, by rising and looking at me."

I did rise, but I could not meet her face: I hid my head on her shoulder; reproducing her action at the time of my own wicked treachery. She did not withdraw it from me, but allowed me to sob there for a minute or two without speaking. She then continued, gently, "You must not doubt either of us, Maria. For myself, your silence about . . . . about Fred, has only produced a temporary inconvenience. And as for your marriage, it is you who have been the sufferer, poor girl. You who have taken the anguish yourself and saved me :—Mr. Latrobe has just told us all, and I shudder to think of what you have gone through. And you have saved me too," Helen added after a short pause, " for a better and happier lot,—if I ever can be happy again,—than

even that once promised. I am engaged to Mr.
Latrobe, Maria."

" Thank Heaven for that at least," I murmured.

" As to Charles," Helen continued, "you have
his full and free forgiveness. He had more difficulty
in pardoning the wrong he thought you had done
me, poor fellow, than in anything else; but I have
quite satisfied him as to that. For himself, you
know, as he says, that you are in no way responsible
for what has occurred. It was God's will that it
should be so, and not your act. On the contrary,
you have been travelling night and day to prevent
any mischief happening; and indeed, indeed, it has
been too much for your strength. See, how you are
trembling now."

" Helen," I whispered, still without looking up,
" may I see him ? That is why I am trembling so.
Oh! Helen, you do not know all: Mr. Latrobe of
course did not mention that. Helen, I loved him
so ! So deeply ! Neither he nor you could ever
have guessed it; least of all when I made that
shameful marriage. I hardly knew it myself; or
rather I would not know it: I was determined to
marry. But now, . . . oh! Helen, my heart is

breaking with it! May I not see him: see him once more?"

Helen hesitated. "If it would not be wrong," she said. . . .

"It cannot be wrong," I interrupted passionately. "It has the seal of death upon it: it is a parting for ever here; and, alas! for hereafter too, perhaps! Helen, let me go back with you! Not for us to meet face to face," I continued; "I could not bear that. Let me stand somewhere in the room where I can see Charles without his seeing me: see but the place he lies on, hear but his voice; but once only: just once more! Helen, say I may come!"

"Come then," Helen answered. "Follow me into the room very softly; for he had fallen asleep just before I left him. I will place you where you can do as you wish. Maria," she added, in a low voice, as we went upstairs, "I did guess something of what you have told me. I used to think how happy and pleasant it would be, if that should ever come off: if he should like you as much as I did. Ah! Maria, I do pity you with all my heart: I do, indeed."

In the next minute, we had entered the room.

Mr. Latrobe expressed some surprise at my appearance with Helen, but did not oppose it. The
room was large, and there was a second bedstead
in it, on the other side of which I was screened
from Charles' view, while I could hear all that
passed. Presently, I arranged the curtains so that I
could see him also ; still without discovering myself.

How that face wrung my heart ! That manly,
but young fair face ! How pallid : soiled in places
with blood and dust : the visible hand of the destroyer
upon it !

He continued sleeping for a minute or two, and
then awoke with a slight tremor ; quickly subsiding
into the calmness which the surgeon regarded as so
unfavourable a symptom.

" Come here, Leenie dear," he said, seeing Helen
in the room. " You have seen her : have said what
I told you ? "

" Yes, Charles."

" That is done then. And now, Leenie," he
continued, raising himself so as to lean on the
pillows of the bed, and putting his hands on both
hers, " you and Mr. Latrobe have not said it to me ;
no more has the doctor. But I have read it in all

your faces : and I had said it to myself long before.
My time has come to die, Leenie : there is something
within me which tells me so. I do not feel particularly ill at present; but I feel *that*. Kiss me,
darling, and don't grieve so much : not more than
you can help."

Charles fondly embraced his sister, whose tears
flowed fast, in spite of all her efforts to restrain them.
He was stroking down her long fair hair with his
hand, as he used to do.

"Do not grieve, Leenie," he said. "It is very
solemn to feel that it is coming so near : everything
seems so real. But I have been praying to One who,
you know, intercedes for us all, Leenie ; and I think
he has heard me : I feel happy, with all the awe.
But I have something to say to Mr. Latrobe, dear,
without your being present : it is the only thing that
troubles me at all. If he can assure me about that,
I shall be quite at rest. You will leave us, Leenie,
for five minutes; will you not ? And," he added,
calling her back as she was leaving the room, " you
will promise never to ask him about it afterwards ?
It is no great secret; but you will not ask to know
it ever, will you, Helen dear ? "

" Sacredly and truly not ; upon my word," Helen answered. She then left the room, and Charles called Mr. Latrobe to him. " I am not sure, sir," he said, " whether I have not done wrong about something : I mean, very lately. I have done plenty of wrong before, God knows, without adding to it. All one's school and home sins, all I have done and left undone, seem to rise up in judgment before me now."

" You must look to His Cross," Mr. Latrobe said, gently.

" I do," said Charles. " I try to do so ; and I believe that, guilty as I have been, He will not cast me away from it. But what I wanted to say to you is something about this trial. I daresay you wondered why I did not say I was not guilty in court, and before the magistrates : although to be sure," Charles added, " you must then have thought that I *was* guilty; and so must every one else. I was astonished myself to see how very clear the proofs seemed ; especially as I could not recollect anything about that handkerchief. But now, now that you know how it all was, you will probably think I ought to have said I was innocent. And that is what I want to ask you about. Was it wrong; was it a sin? You know that, as I told you at the time, great idiot that I was, I thought Helen had done it then;—not knowing what she was doing, of course, but in delirium or something: quite without fault of her own. And I could not bear the thought of her lying under such a charge when I found I could take it on myself. But I am fearful now that this may not have been right. I told no untruth about it; but I ought to have gone beyond this: I ought to have simply stated my innocence, and left her in safer and wiser hands. I should not like to die without having repented of this, if it was a sin."

"Charles! Charles!" said Mr. Latrobe, in an agony of grief, "you break my heart! Oh! my God," he exclaimed, turning aside, as he thus received the confirmation of the surmise which had broken upon him in court that morning, "if such sins need forgiveness, what must become of the good deeds of the rest of us!"

It was some time before Mr. Latrobe could recover himself sufficiently to reply to Charles' question; but the evident anxiety of the latter made him feel the necessity of doing so.

"I certainly think, Charles," he said at length, "that you did wrong, in one sense ; but I venture to tell you, as the minister of religion, that you need not burden your conscience with further uneasiness on this score. The error, at the utmost, was one of judgment, not of will ; and where the motive was such as yours, we may trust that our merciful Redeemer will pardon greater offences than this. You may reflect too, for your comfort, that, even if you had protested your innocence, the result would probably have been the same : no asseveration of yours would have been sufficient to rebut the apparent proofs of your crime."

"Thank you, sir ; thank you deeply," said Charles. "You have lifted a heavy weight from my mind. And now, Mr. Latrobe, will you call Helen, please : but stay," he added, "you must first promise, as she has done, that she is never told of this. Poor child, she will be in sad grief for me, in any case ; and this would only make it worse."

The curate gave the required assurance : very unwillingly ; but he felt it impossible to refuse Charles's request.

Helen re-entered the room soon afterwards.

Already, it seemed to her, a marked alteration had taken place in the figure which lay, half propped, half reclining, on the bed : the power of support seemed less ; the reclining more necessary. Already the coma, the final and fatal signal, had set in.

Charles's voice too was altered. Hitherto, even under the painful circumstances of the last few hours, it had retained something of its old cheery ring ; it was now feebler, less distinct in tone : sounded like the same voice at a distance. He did not in fact speak for a minute or two after Helen's return.

"Leenie, dear," he then said, "come and sit down by me here : on this chair. I feel so weak, as if I wanted somebody to hold me. I was thinking of our Harrow eleven just when you came in ; I don't know why. Poor old cricket-field ! I shouldn't make much of an innings there now, I fancy."

Then there was another pause. Once more Charles seemed to sleep ; but soon he again roused himself, although with a perceptible effort. "I have been wandering," he said : "this drowsy fit has been upon me again. I cannot think much ; not as I ought to at this time. Leenie, dearest, I wish you would sing me something ;—one of those hymns

that Mamma used to sing on Sunday evenings: I
could attend to that. There was one about some
one . . . about the shadows. Don't you recollect,
Leenie ? "

" Yes, Charles."

" Sing that, dear."

Solemnly and sweetly, forcing back its sobs,
Helen's voice rose in the chamber of death. The
pilgrim-psalm of the spirit parting for its long
exile !

> " Faint not when thy strength is less,
> Heed not the heart's weariness ;
> Fear not for the dark wayside,
> Where the lengthening shadows glide ;
> Journey with no doubtful tread
> To the land unvisited.
>
> Wakes for thee the angel spear,
> Breathes for thee the Comforter ;
> Mercy hears thee in each cry
> Of thy soul's mute agony ;
> Through the barred and vaulted tomb
> Opens the eternal home."

Helen's voice ceased, but Charles made no answer.
Again he slept, long and heavily : very long, very
heavily, this time. His breathing was regular in
its periods, but unnatural ; the loaded, stertorous
breathing of the over-mastered brain. It seemed
as if this must be the end.

But nature roused itself once more: or rather the loving heart did. Shaking off his drowsiness Charles lifted himself, almost by force, on his elbow and looked round. "Mr. Latrobe," he said: "Helen! where are you ?"

"Here, Charles," said Helen; "close to you. Do not you see us ?"

No. The sight had become dim now.

"I cannot see you. Leenie, dear, put your arm round me: do not take it away. I can feel you, at any rate. Where is Mr. Latrobe?"

"Here, Charles," the curate answered: "standing by your sister."

"Mr. Latrobe, there is one other thing I have thought about. It is very odd how I go on sleeping and thinking of things at the same time. It is about her; Miss Secretan, you know."

"Yes, Charles."

"I can't recollect all you told me; I am so confused now. But I remember that."

"That?" asked the curate.

"Yes: when she found it all out: found that Mr. Fortescue had done it. She ought to have come forward at once, you know, and cleared

Helen; but she didn't: not for some weeks afterwards. Mr. Latrobe, that must not be known."

"It may be impossible to avoid it," said Mr. Latrobe gently. "I will do what I can to further any wish of hers about it, but . . . "

"*Her* wish," said Charles interrupting him. "That will only be to condemn herself; to publish what she has done wrong to all the world. She is generous, fearless, in her real character: I often saw it, before all that happened. You will grant me this last request, Mr. Latrobe? You will tell her herself, that it was my last wish?"

As Charles spoke, I sprang forward from my place of concealment with a loud cry: the old heart-broken cry of all those days; "Oh! Charles, Charles!" I could forbear no longer. What was seeing him, hearing him? I must speak to him with my own lips. Must claim my share—my share too, in the few last sands of the life which was now running so low!

But it was too late. My own approach, as well as the reply which Mr. Latrobe had been about to make were simultaneously arrested by the same cause. A startling change passed over Charles's face. The eye suddenly glazed ; the head sunk back on the pillow ; the heavy breathing of the death-coma recommenced. And this time, with no awakening.

With no awakening. But with an end, brief now, and painless. Indicating only by a gentle sigh the moment when the mortal and the transitory passed into the undying and eternal.

CHAPTER XVII.

SOMETHING remains to be told ere I can finally draw the veil over this record of a great misery. A few pages only. And then my task will be complete.

It had been arranged that my deposition as to the circumstances under which Frederick Poynder's death had really occurred should be taken as soon as possible. At an early hour on the day following that of which I have just written, I accompanied Mr. Rigwell and Mr. Latrobe before the magistrates for that purpose.

Before the attorney joined us, Mr. Latrobe had extracted from me a promise that I would comply with the wish expressed by Charles in his last moments, and would not disclose, unless it should become absolutely necessary, my own wrong-doing in the matter. Most reluctantly was the promise given. In my present state of feeling, it appeared intolerable that I should suppress this : I longed to publish my shame, my guilt, in the broadest daylight. It seemed the only healing :—some reparation, slight as it might have been, for a crime so hateful in itself, so disastrous in its results. But Mr. Latrobe urged upon me the sacredness of this parting request, and I consented to do as Charles had wished. In my own heart, I hoped that something might occur in the course of the deposition, which would compel my statement of this unhappy fact among the rest.

This however proved not to be the case. I detailed the main particulars as I had done to Mr. Latrobe the evening before : recapitulated my husband's narrative ; produced the steel cross which he had taken from the child's neck, and the implement with which the fatal wound had been inflicted ; explained how Charles's handkerchief had come into Mr. Fortescue's possession ; lastly, mentioned my having accidentally heard of Charles's committal on the charge, and my immediate return to England in consequence.

The story was listened to with breathless astonishment by all present. But it was fully and immediately credited. It would have been so, even had not Mr. Rigwell, whose deposition was also taken, supplied the ample evidence which he had procured in corroboration of it. As regarded my own part in the matter, no suspicion of anything amiss seemed to occur to those present. It was easily intelligible that, although possessed of the secret, I should have forborne to criminate Mr. Fortescue : at any rate, until some other person was charged with it; and no question was asked as to my knowledge of Helen's committal on the charge, or the time at which I had left for the Continent.

Alas ! no. Far from the bench suspecting the suppression of which I had been guilty, I was actually complimented by them ! They spoke of my promptitude and generosity; of my having at once, on hearing of Charles's committal, undertaken so exhausting a journey in order to establish his innocence, and make a disclosure which could not but be so painful to myself; of their regret at the disaster which had prevented my efforts being successful, although it could not detract from their merit ! Ah ! me. My woe ; my woe !

And thus terminated all judicial dealing with the

matter, excepting as regarded the proceedings arising
out of the riot of the day before; and those which
would be grounded upon Mr. Rigwell's and my
depositions, in the event of Mr. Fortescue returning
to England. For the present treaties under which
criminals are liable to arrest abroad, did not then
exist.

In Helen's case the indictment was at once with-
drawn, and she was released from confinement; the
magistrates, as well as the grand jury, stating their
conviction that the innocence both of herself and
Charles was established in the fullest manner, and
adding an expression of their profound sympathy at
the catastrophe in which the charge against the latter
had resulted. It is needless to say that the sentiment
was powerfully responded to by the public at large.

Thus, as I have said, the matter terminated in its
external aspect. The mourners were left alone.

And they were soon parted, also. On quitting
the magistrates' room I returned to a sitting-room
which Mr. Latrobe had engaged for me at the hotel.
Here Helen came to me, shortly after her discharge
was made out, and took leave of me for the present;
it having been arranged that she should return to

Hastings under Mr. Latrobe's escort, and come back for Charles's funeral.

" Farewell till then," Helen said, as we mingled our tears.

Ah ! The farewell was for ever !

The chaise drove off with her and Mr. Latrobe, and I was left in my sitting-room alone. How alone ! How alone ! A sense of utter desolation fell upon me. Something too withering, not for mere grief, mere penitence only, but for thought itself. I sat in the room for hours, motionless, purposeless ; unconscious of the place, of the lapse of time, of everything.

Unconscious, so far as its conveying any definite idea to the brain went : of something which my ear took in mechanically. A sound of wheels driving up hurriedly to the hotel door, followed by some bustle in the hall below ; the tread of several footsteps in the passage outside my room ; the steps suddenly ceasing, at a call from below ;—returning downstairs. Then, after an interval, other footsteps : those of one person only this time. A long pause at my door ; then a knock, gentle and hesitating : another knock and another, as I made no reply. Then the

door softly opened. Some one entering; standing
in front of me ; holding out something for me
to take.

A letter ? Yes.

Mechanically, as before, I saw this : saw that it
bore a foreign post-mark ; was sealed and edged
with black ; was in a writing of which I had no
knowledge. Saw that the person who was presenting
it was the proprietor of the hotel, who had spoken to
me the evening before on my arrival : heard him
speak to me now.

" Mrs. Fortescue, I believe," he said.

I inclined my head, doubtless: I was not conscious
that I did so.

" I must apologise for thus intruding upon you,
madam," he continued, " but I did not like to keep
this without its at once reaching your hand. It has
just arrived here ; it was forwarded, according to
instructions given to the captain of the packet, by a
special messenger from Dover."

Mechanically still, I took the letter; the proprietor bowing as he withdrew, but returning from
the door with a courteous request that I would
command himself and the resources of his house in

any way in which they could be of service. And,
mechanically still, with the outward action of the
hand and eye, but with no distinct impression passing
to the mind from either, I broke the seal, and read as
follows.

" Tavannes, Munster Thal, Switzerland.
—April 18 . .

" MADAM,

" Our landlord, M. Borghers, has requested
me, as the only English visitor here at present, to
inform you of a sad disaster which has overtaken us.
I heartily wish I knew how to discharge the task
better. You must prepare yourself for a great
sorrow : and I have no means of breaking it to you ;
any further than the external indications of this letter
may have done so. You will have guessed that
the hand of death has fallen somewhere ; and, if
you observed the post-mark, you will have feared
that the sufferer may have been your husband,
Mr. Fortescue. He died yesterday evening, from a
second, and fatal access of paralysis ; the result of
his own noble conduct on the previous night, when
the hotel here, at which you have recently been
staying with him, was totally destroyed by fire ; and
when he exerted himself in saving life with a heroism

and self-devotion which must aggravate his loss to you in one sense, although at the same time it cannot fail to afford you consolation under it.

"You will be anxious to hear the details of this calamitous occurrence. I can only give them as far as my personal observation went, for the village has been one scene of confusion ever since, and it is impossible to extract a connected account from any one. My wife (Mrs. Stewart) and myself had been out on a mountain ramble all day, and did not return to the hotel until past seven on the night of the fire; just in time for supper. We were both tired, and went early to our bedroom, which was on the top floor of the hotel. The latter, you will probably recollect, was built of wood, excepting the basement, and of a great height;—four stories, with an attic above, for domestics. Our room was on the fourth story.

"From the time of our going to bed, which was about ten o'clock, I remember nothing until I was awakened by Mrs. Stewart. She told me there was a strong smell of fire, and wished me to get up and see if anything was the matter. I was sleeping heavily, and lay on at first, half awake and half dozing, assuring her she must be mistaken. Several minutes must have been lost in this way. In the meantime however the smell had become unmistakeable, and my wife insisted on my rousing myself. I did so, and ran to the door of the room, which I opened. A volume of smoke at once rushed in, and I saw that the lower part of the staircase was in flames, precluding all escape that way.

" Our only chance was the window; and this seemed a poor one, from its great height. There was no time for consideration however; and having a general idea what to do in an emergency of the kind, I flung out the mattresses from our own bed, and from a second one which was in the room; Mrs. Stewart meanwhile, by my direction, had been tearing the sheets into strips, and by these we eventually descended unhurt, although a good deal shaken; the bedding having broken our fall. A nephew of mine, who was sleeping two stories below us, was less fortunate. He jumped from the window on the first alarm, and I fear will be a cripple for life.

" I have gone into these personal details, because you will naturally wish to know all that can be told about this disaster; and unfortunately, as I have

said, I can obtain no particulars of it excepting those
which thus came within my own knowledge :—of the
origin of the fire no one seems to have the least
conception. Let me now hasten to speak of your
lamented husband.

"As soon as I could recover myself from the
shock of my fall, I hastened to render every assistance in my power. It was at once obvious that to
save the building was hopeless. Sheets of flame
darted from every window in the front ;—that which,
as you may remember, faced the valley, and the main
street of the village. If we could have poured the
whole river upon the building, it would have been
too late. Already the glow of the fire was seen in
the rooms at right angles to the front, overlooking
the road up to the church ; although they had not
actually caught as yet. The fabric, at any rate its
upper portion, was hopelessly doomed.

" This being so, our only concern was the preser-
vation of life. In this I found your brave husband
had anticipated me. There were very few visitors in
the hotel, fortunately ; the season not having commenced :—our own occupation of the upper rooms
was the result of choice, from the exquisite view they

commanded. For the most part too the inmates had been awakened in time, and had escaped with little injury. Two families however had been less fortunate : one that of the landlord of the hotel; the other visitors ;—Germans. Both had been overlooked in the confusion. The Germans, an elderly gentleman, with his son and son's wife, occupying two adjoining bedrooms, seemed not to have woke, and were possibly now stupefied by the smoke. The landlord's family consisted of two persons ; his eldest daughter, a girl of sixteen, and an infant of a few months old : the mother was not living. Hurrying down stairs on the first alarm of fire, to ascertain the extent of the mischief, the landlord had left his daughter hastily dressing herself, and preparing to follow him with the child immediately ; and there was no difficulty in their doing so, as their room was on the first floor, and the staircase from it, like all the basement, was stone : in fact the fire had not then reached so far. But this party also were nowhere visible among those outside. It was feared that they must have taken some wrong turning, and be at that very time, if not a prey to the flames, hopelessly wandering about the building.

" Of these circumstances Mr. Fortescue had already apprised himself before I came up. His appearance on the spot struck me with the greatest astonishment. I was aware of his serious illness; and that although he was recovered from this, it had still left him quite the invalid;—he had never joined the *table-d'hôte*, for instance, and whenever we had met him out walking it was always with the support of a stick.

" Knowing this, it was with extreme surprise that I saw your husband, just where one would wish an Englishman to be, standing in front of the villagers, who were either looking on helplessly or throwing some jets of water from a small fire-engine which did more harm than good, and persuading them to lend their efforts to his assistance in trying to save the lives which were known to be in danger. Still more was I amazed at the personal strength and activity which he displayed. From the bed of paralysis,—as in fact does at times happen with this disorder—he had risen into the possession of powers in which few men, in their fullest health and vigour, could have equalled him. Before I reached him, he had already organized a plan for rescuing the Germans, who were on the second floor. This was fairly seconded by the villagers, into whom he had infused some portion of his own marvellous energy; and within a few minutes I had the satisfaction of seeing this family, who on waking up at length and seeing nothing but smoke and flame round them had given themselves up for lost, brought down to the street in safety.

"There remained the other, and still more piteous case; that of the landlord's two children. I felt in a moment Mr. Fortescue's superior claim to direct, and told him that I would take my part in executing whatever he could devise for their relief.

"Unhappily, our efforts seemed fruitless. Nothing could be seen or heard of this unfortunate party from the outside; and the only doors in the building were now hopelessly blocked by the flames. Mr. Fortescue's eye however was caught by a tree, adjoining the only angle of the hotel to which the fire had not yet penetrated. It seemed the work of a moment for him to ascend this to a point opposite the first floor; one of the windows of which was open, although apparently at a hopeless distance from the branch to which he had climbed. He made the leap however, and with entire success; and then immediately disappeared within; having previously directed me to remain near the window, in the event of his being able to rescue any one from the interior.

" Several most anxious minutes passed, and then I again heard Mr. Fortescue's voice above me. He had found the two children at no great distance, crouched on the landing-place of a staircase, the upper part of which was already in flames, and anticipating death every moment. It was in vain however that we endeavoured to discover any mode of passing them to the ground. There was no bedding in the room he had entered, or in the adjoining ones; it was a new wing, lately added, and had not yet been furnished. I sent messenger after messenger for a ladder, but none came. The daughter meanwhile, carrying the younger child in her arms, had followed him into the room, and stood by his side at the window in speechless terror. The flames had entered the room with the girl; they were already visible from the outside. Nothing could have escaped through *them* with life.

" ' It must be done,' Mr. Fortescue exclaimed on seeing this. ' There is no other way.'

" As he spoke, he took off his own coat, and

gently and carefully wrapping the infant in it, and lowering himself from the window with one hand, held his burden with the other, until he was able to drop it at the nearest distance to the ground. The child's fall was greatly broken by these precautions, and as I had it in my arms almost before it had touched the ground, it escaped with no injury. Mr. Fortescue meanwhile had returned to the sister. He seemed for a moment to be considering whether he could lower her in the same way : but it was hopeless, even for his astonishing strength. He then sat down on the window-sill, and entreating his companion to give herself entirely up to him, placed her in a sitting posture, clasped her tightly to him, with both arms, and then, raising one foot, sprung from the window.

" The poor girl's life was saved, but her deliverer had sacrificed his own. I immediately ran to him, and found him lying stunned and motionless. Having myself some knowledge of medicine, I adopted the best means I could for restoring animation, and was partially successful. His eyes unclosed, and he spoke a few words; but so indistinctly that I was wholly unable to catch their import.

"In another minute, the hand of a more fatal enemy was upon him. The paralysis returned with augmented force, and he sunk into total unconsciousness; which continued until he breathed his last, as I have already stated, late yesterday evening: about nine o'clock.

"I make no apology for the length of this letter; indeed, I only regret my inability to give you further details. I fear that the interment must take place before it is possible that you should arrive, and I have taken on myself to make the necessary arrangements for it. It will be a privilege, although a melancholy one, to follow to their last resting-place the remains of one whose noble, self-sacrificing heroism has awakened an almost enthusiastic reverence in the minds of those who witnessed it, and will long survive in the simple records of this valley.

"I am, Madam,

"With very sincere sympathy,

"Your obedient servant,

"JAMES L. STEWART."

So, not at the last unhappily, had passed from earth this other life; involved, from no fault of its own, in so mysterious and fatal a tragedy!

And so, too, had terminated my own short-lived dream of ambition! Could I have foreseen, those few months before, when its bright realization first opened upon me, in what utter darkness it would close, I should have shrunk from the forecast with dismay.

Ah! it brought with it no such feeling now! Neither regret, nor disappointment, nor even remorse. My heart was full: it had but one utterance. The cry of my self-blighted love: the old cry:—" Oh, Charles, Charles ! "

  *   *   *   *   *   *

And here my tale might close ; for its eventful portion is at an end. But the reader may wish that it should contain some short further notice of those with whom it has been so long conversant.

Let such particulars as I have to give, stand in a new—and final—chapter. Let them stand, as other portions of my story have done, in the language and with the current emotions and thoughts of those from whose narration I received them; and not in the sombre surroundings of my own life.

CHAPTER XVIII.

It was some two years after the events related in the last chapter, on a pleasant April afternoon, that a clergyman and his young wife drove up the gravel sweep to their rectory door. The rectory was in Somersetshire;—a charming house, looking one way down a grass valley to the spires of the market-town from which they had just returned in the pony-chaise, and looking up, in the opposite direction, to a curve of hill and rich meadow-land, on the lower slope of which the stately church-tower, the parsonage, and the thatched cottages were now basking in the spring sunshine.

"Hallo!" said the incumbent, as they turned a corner of the shrubbery which brought them in view of their own door. "What fly is that? Have you any idea, Helen?"

"None whatever," replied Mrs. Latrobe. For the incumbent, if the Clergy list gave his name correctly, was Jean Hyacinthe Latrobe ; and Helen was now his wife : had been for some months.

"Visitors, I suppose," said Mr. Latrobe. "Who can they be? Well, we're in for it now. What is there for lunch, my dear?"

"Only the pie, and vegetables; but Reeves can do some chops, if they stop: I don't suppose they will."

"Ask them, at any rate," said Mr. Latrobe, entering the hall, where he was met by a pleasant-faced handy parlour-maid.

"If you please, sir, there are a gentleman and lady in the drawing-room. I asked them to sit down, as they seemed disappointed at not finding you : they gave these cards, if you please, sir."

Mr. Latrobe glanced at a singularly small and neat piece of pasteboard on which was printed, "Mr. S. Partridge, Hastings." Accompanying this was a card correspondingly large in its proportions, with the name, "Mrs. Partridge."

And when Mr. Latrobe and Helen entered the drawing-room, they discovered that the gentleman

was one of whom the reader has some previous knowledge as a resident at Hastings; and that Mrs.
Partridge was their former acquaintance : then, in her
widowed condition, Mrs. Graves.

"How very charming, Mrs. . . .," Mr. Latrobe
began. "Ah!" he added laughing, "I was just
going to give you your old name: only think!
Well, Mr. Partridge, I do congratulate you with all
my heart."

"Thank you, sir, I won't say to the contrary,"
answered Mr. Partridge, who was as dry-spoken
as ever.

"I should think not indeed! And when did it
come off, Mrs. . . I mean, my dear Mrs. Partridge ?
We have not seen it in the papers."

The bride simpered a little, and then broke into
one of her former hearty laughs. "It was only two
days ago, Mr. Latrobe. We thought we'd leave the
public in their ignorance just for a week or so: it's
an excellent plan. They charge you double for everything at the hotels if they know about it :—spoons
extra, as my poor . . . ."

"Hindoo widow," interposed Mr. Partridge,
laconically.

" All right, my dear."

Mr. Latrobe looked from one speaker to the other in some amazement ; but seeing nothing to explain this by-play, concluded it to be some form of love-passage between the parties, and resumed.

" Well, *we* know the secret, at any rate. And now, my dear Mrs. Partridge, you and your husband must positively spend a day or two with us : you shall have the large spare room, ' elaborately furnished in the newest style,' as the house-agents say."

" Greatly obleeged, sir," said Mr. Partridge ; " but we are going on to Yeovil this afternoon : I have a business appointment there to-morrow."

" Indeed ! " said Mr. Latrobe.

" Yes ; isn't it just like him, Mr. Latrobe ? " said the wife. " I thought he'd have taken us to Bath, or some such place ; not to a stupid market-town, where there's nothing but pigs and ploughs. But he'd got this business, so he thought he would kill two birds with one stone : and I'm obliged to submit," said the ex-widow, resignedly.

" Of course you are, Mrs. Partridge," Mr. Latrobe answered. " Well, thank you for coming to see us, at any rate ; and we shall have lunch in punctually at two.   Where did you come from to-day ? "

" Marlborough," said Mr. Partridge.

" Yes, Mr. Latrobe," said his wife ; " and I hope it's the last time I shall ever set foot there. What do you think they did at the hotel ? Quite early this morning, not seven o'clock I should think, we were woke up by a noise at our window, and found there was a plumber painter and glazier's man, with a white cap, putting in a new pane. Never can think what they wear those paper caps for. I recollect my. . . ."

" Hindoo widow," again interposed Mr. Partridge.

" All right, Mr. Partridge," said his wife.

Helen rose from her chair, saying she would go to see about lunch ; but whispered to Mr. Latrobe as she passed him, " Do you think he's lost his senses ? "

" Don't know I'm sure, my dear," replied Mr. Latrobe, whose dismay was equal to her own, in the same key.   " Well, come, now, Mrs. Partridge," he said, aloud, " while they are laying the cloth you shall tell us about our Hastings acquaintances.   We have not heard of them for a long time."

" I don't know that there's any particular news,"

said Mrs. Partridge.   " You have heard of the rector's
death, I daresay ? "

" Yes, I saw it in the Times."

" It was bronchitis, at the last," said Mrs.
Partridge.   " ' Assisted by Mr. Sims ; '   only the
doctors won't let them put *that* in as they do the
clergyman in the marriage advertisements.   That's
what my blessed departed . . ."

" Hindoo widow," said Mr. Partridge once more,
striking out the words like a clock-hammer.

" Yes, yes," said his wife, with some little ex-
asperation ; " how you do tease one.   I daresay you
wonder," she added, recovering her good-humour the
next instant, and addressing Mr. Latrobe, whose
perplexity was now extreme,—" I daresay you wonder
what that is he is saying.   It's only a little arrangement between us.   He thinks I talk too much about
poor Mr. Graves : at least he told me so soon after
we were engaged.   He said it didn't sound well now
I was about to enter on the holy state again.   ' It
would be another thing,' he said, ' if you'd been a
Hindoo widow.   You'd have jumped into the fire
after him once for all then, and there'd have been
an end of it.'   ' Very well,' I said.   ' When you

think I'm coming to it, then you say 'Hindoo widow' to me, and I'll stop if I can.' "

"A most ingenious plan, really," said Mr. Latrobe. "By the way, how is Mr. Sims? And Mr. Rigwell too? I have not heard either of their names since we left Hastings."

"Both thriving, Mr. Latrobe," said his visitor. "Of course," she added in a lowered voice, although Helen was still out of the room, "of course you know about Mrs. Armitage?"

"No, indeed, Mrs. Partridge. There is the connection between us, no doubt; but the circumstances were very painful, and it was felt best, on both sides, that there should be no attempt to keep up any correspondence. What about her?"

"It's a sad story enough, poor woman," said Mrs. Partridge, "but I fear there is no doubt about the facts. As I need not tell you, she came into possession of a very handsome income on Mr. Armitage's death, quite at her own disposal. She went abroad with the two girls; and, at some foreign watering-place, fell in with an Hungarian count, as he called himself, who paid her a great deal of attention, and at last persuaded her to marry him."

"Indeed!" said Mr. Latrobe; "I had no suspicion of this. I fear from what you say that she was imposed upon."

"Most grossly," said his visitor. "It was speedily discovered that her husband was an Englishman all the time; a Londoner; it is even said that he had been a billiard-marker at the West End. Poor thing! whatever he was, he used her badly enough. She had made no settlement upon herself, and the first thing he did was to raise the full value upon her life income, which was at his mercy as soon as they married."

"I am very grieved," said Mr. Latrobe. "Is she still living with him?"

"Oh! no," said Mrs. Partridge. "I am afraid he treated her shamefully during the few days they were together; but then he disappeared altogether, leaving her penniless. She was able to get back to England; and now some relatives of her first husband have taken in herself and the two girls. I am very sorry for them."

Here however the lunch-bell rang, breaking off the conversation. Nor must I abuse the reader's patience by resuming it.

Of Mr. Latrobe and Helen little further need
be said. Mr. Latrobe was now, in right of his wife,
a rich man; for with the exception of the life income
secured to Mrs. Armitage, and alienated by her
as just mentioned, the whole of Mr. Armitage's handsome fortune had devolved upon Helen.

That neither of them were spoilt by affluence; that
Mr. Latrobe, when not occupied by his parish—and
there was a hamlet of brick-burners some two miles off
which gave him more occupation than its rural character
might have seemed to promise—did not batten in
idleness, but worked hard in the furtherance of every
project, local or remote, which could reclaim error,
or alleviate suffering; that Helen, admired and
welcomed everywhere, prized no welcome like that
of the humble homes which her eye and voice cheered
even more than her money:—of all this the reader
will not require to be told.

Not of this. Nor of that one grief, which, even
after many years have elapsed, still remains to temper
a happiness which might otherwise have seemed
too complete. Still, and always, a grief; and yet
one so near akin to a joy that it would need a cunning
hand to map out the line of separation. When the

Offertory Prayer is read in church, Mr. Latrobe involuntarily pauses over its closing sentence, recalling that young life, snatched from earth so early, and yet bequeathing to it a memory of such undying brightness. There is a little miniature of Charles in their room, done shortly before his leaving Harrow; —rude enough; merely the face, with its frank boyish look, not disfigured by outrage and suffering as they had last seen it;—and yet no saint of Raphael's was ever tended with such reverence. There is a small room adjoining theirs; Charles's room, as it is always called; the reproduction of his own at Hastings; books, gun, fishing-tackle, pictures; all arranged as he left them: all but speaking and moving images of himself. There is his name, never banished; never forgotten; not often pronounced, but then never sadly.

And last of all, there is his secret: the one secret between husband and wife. Still faithfully kept: no betrayal on the one part; no unauthorized query on the other. I know not if Helen guesses it. I think she does;—think she guessed it from the first. But if she does, or did, she could not love him better. Love him with a better love than that which will not admit its loss, because it retains the reality of possession.

And now I have written of all but myself.

And of myself?

A very few words may suffice for this. They are scarce worth the saying, but my heart yearns to utter them.

My dream was over: it had lasted a short six months. The waking had come, and it was to last through an entire life.

I returned to Switzerland. To Tavannes,—the scene of Mr. Fortescue's death,—first of all; then further south. The generosity of the distant kinsman who succeeded to the Dalemain estates secured me an income, more than sufficient for my wants; far more than I had either hoped or merited. With this I retired to a small *pension* in one of the upper valleys opening out of that by which the Rhone descends to the Lake of Geneva. I engaged apartments there for a few weeks. I have occupied them, with the exception of one or two brief visits to England, up to the present time :—many years now after the conclusion of my tale, and when even its known incidents have long ceased to exist in public memory. Of the darker secret connected with them, no one, excepting the two persons of whom I have lastly written, has ever heard; or will hear, until the publication of this history after my death.

The poor peasantry among whom I live, and whom I endeavour to benefit as far as I may, are friendly, unobtrusive, tolerant of my loneliness and self-seclusion. That there is some heavy grief in which the English lady has borne a part they doubtless guess; but they make no attempt to inquire into it: and no visitors from my own country ever find their way here. There is no carriage-road within miles; nothing to attract pedestrians. A difficult and dreary pass skirts the head of the valley, without dipping into it. But few tourists take this route; and those who do, hasten from the desolation which surrounds them to the security of the lower pastures.

So I wander about alone; wander, as I used to do at Hastings. Not so far now; for grief has told upon me even more than years. Not with that fair prospect before me, gorse-covered cliff and blue sea and jutting headland; but amid scenes of gloom and sterility. On few days in the year does the sun ever penetrate to the upper part of this valley. On one

side glaciers frown over it; on the other rises a
mountain, lofty and precipitous, but shattered to its
summit by some former convulsion of nature, and
impending ominously over the vale-head. Of its five
peaks, three have already fallen; the other two
momentarily threaten the same catastrophe, blanch-
ing the cheek and quickening the step of the traveller
who skirts their base. Darkness and barrenness:
darkness and barrenness; without and within. Ah!
I have well earned both!

Nor do they trouble me, now. Not even my
sorrow of sorrows, my self-profaned love, does that
now: not often. Time has brought healing to that
also.

But can it, can anything, heal the real malady?
That heavy, heavy guilt which I bear about with me;
which scares me in those ruinous peaks, makes voices
-for me in the desolation of that marred valley; haunts
me, at all times, everywhere, with an evil presence,
the forecast of a worse doom!

Heaven be praised, Yes. Not yet: not yet. Not
in time at all. I shall not have the time. My life is
not long past its prime, even now; but no life can go
through the emotions which mine has, and remain

unimpaired.　Something tells me that the end is not now far off : tells me, at the same time, that the end may not be—despair !

Even as I have penned the self-accusation of these pages, a weight seems lifted from me.　The same scenes : the same gloomy imageries; but not, as before, all gloom.

In the mountain-rift, the thunder, the avalanche, I still read the Judge.　In the spring-flowers, in soft airs and brightened skies, in the chant of village-worshippers rising from the lowly church, I see, I hear, the Absolver !

Not in vain, even to erring man himself, has that power of remitting sin been delegated.　Not in vain has that Cross been lifted which alone taketh away the sins of the world !

FINIS.

London : Printed by SMITH, ELDER and Co., Old Bailey, E.C.

www.ingramcontent.com/pod-product-compliance
Lightning Source LLC
Chambersburg PA
CBHW020850020726
47497CB00005B/1338